The nurses quickly got Allyson ready to go to surgery. She clutched my hand and in a hushed voice, she said, "Kelly, if I die, I want you to know—"

"Ally, you aren't going to die!" I cried. "You can't die!"

She put her hand over my lips. "Shh. I want you to know how much I love you, Little Sister."

My throat got so tight I could hardly speak. We clung to each other for a minute, then the nurses came to take her to surgery. She gave my hand a little squeeze. But her eyes were looking off somewhere else and I don't even think she saw us anymore. She seemed to be off in her own world. And none of us could follow her there.

Is this the last time I'll ever see her? I wondered.

If you want to know more about kidney disease and kidney transplants, you can write to:

American Kidney Fund
6110 Executive Blvd.
Rockville, MD 20852

National Kidney Foundation
2 Park Avenue
New York, NY 10016

Is My Sister DYING?

by Alida E. Young

I would like to dedicate this book to all the people who work in the field of organ transplants, and to the donors, who truly give the gift of life.

Very special thanks for all their help to Mikki Masteller, R.N., B.S.N., Sharon Robie, R.N., Sandy Teichman, R.N., Liz Ramirez, R.N., Administrator of Palm Desert Dialysis Center, Michael Cervantes, L.C.S.W., Sandra Laskill, Licensed Nutritionist, Edgar Gambia, M.D., Desiree Benoit, Joslyn Wiles, Kay Bassford, Vicka Carillo, Marco Holbrook, J. Arthur Robinson, Bookseller, of Yucca Valley, CA, the American Kidney Fund, and the National Kidney Foundation.

Published by Willowisp Press, Inc.
10100 SBF Drive, Pinellas Park, Florida 34666

Copyright © 1991 by Willowisp Press, Inc.

Printed in the United States of America

10 9 8 7 6 5 4 3

ISBN   0-87406-541-0

One

"KELLY, isn't this great?" Stephie asked over the blare of the trumpets, sousaphones, and drums of the Corina High marching band. "I love riding in a parade even more than watching one."

I grinned at my best friend and waved to the crowd that lined the street. Stephanie Miller and I belonged to the Boots and Saddles Club. This was our first year to ride our horses in the Labor Day parade. For the last three years I'd had to stand on the sidelines watching my older sister Allyson. Now it was my turn and I loved it.

"I hope my dad gets some good shots of us on the video camera," Stephie said.

I scanned the crowd, looking for our parents. "They're probably waiting near the end of the route," I said. "I just hope my mom and dad haven't left to go show a house."

5

My parents own a real estate company and they work strange hours. Whenever people want to see a house that's for sale, they have to go show it. That's the way their business works. It would be just my luck for them to miss my big moment in the parade.

Allyson had been riding two rows in front of us. She dropped back to be closer to us. Her dapple gray thoroughbred, Airborne, was outfitted in a new jumping saddle and bridle. Grandma Allyson, Dad's mother, gave them to her on her seventeenth birthday.

Airborne walked beside me and Sidekick, my black and tan buckskin quarterhorse. "Well, how does it feel to be in your first parade?" Allyson asked with a big smile. "Never mind. You don't have to answer. I can see by your face."

I nodded. "It's great having everybody waving at you. Does it ever get to be a drag?"

"Never!" Allyson said. "I could ride in the parade until I'm sixty and I'd never get bored with it."

She'll probably look just as good at sixty as she does at seventeen, I thought with a sigh. Ally's into English-style riding and she looks super in her black hunt coat and black velvet helmet. Actually, she looks great in everything. I'd give anything to look like her.

"After the parade, do you and Stephie want to work out at the center?" Allyson asked. "I'm not great at barrel racing, but I could probably give you some pointers. I used to watch Dad race when I was little."

Dad had won lots of competitions before he hurt his leg. After that, he got into selling real estate. "That'd be great," I said. "We need all the help we can get."

"I can't do it today," Stephie said in a disappointed voice. "I have to baby-sit Jonathan."

Jonathan is her one-year-old little brother. There's nothing in the world that Stephie hates more than baby-sitting.

"You don't need much help," Allyson said to Stephie. "Kelly thinks you're a cinch to make the team."

"I sure hope so," Stephie said grinning.

"Well," Allyson said. "I'd better get back to Keith before he thinks I've deserted him. See you at the end of the parade."

Keith Harrison is her boyfriend. I like him a lot because he never treats me like a little kid.

"Boy, you sure have a great sister," Stephie said. She made a face. "I don't suppose you'd like to trade her for a little brother?"

I grinned at her and said, "No way!"

Brian Ackerman, who had been riding right behind us, pulled up beside me.

"Did you know that there is a specific name for a loud parade?" he asked, giving me a triumphant grin. We are both trivia buffs, and we love to stump each other with weird facts.

"You got me," I gave in.

"It's called a *callithump*," he said.

Brian is fifteen, a year older than Stephie and me. He belongs to the same riding club, and all three of us compete in barrel racing. Brian is fun and a little crazy sometimes. You never know what he's going to say or do.

He and I like the same things. He wants to be a veterinarian. I want to be a doctor. We like riding, the same types of music, and horror movies—the more gruesome and gross, the better. We both like to go snorkeling and body surfing at the beach. With all that in common, you'd think he'd ask me to go to a movie or get a pizza or something. He hangs around our house a lot, but it's because he has a crush on Allyson.

The parade moved ahead. The morning sun poked through the clouds. I waved and smiled to all the people, wishing I could be in a parade every day.

"What's the matter with your sister?" Brian asked. "She's not sitting right in the saddle."

Big deal, I thought. So Allyson wasn't sitting up straight. If *I* was slouching in my saddle, would he notice? I doubted it. But then I wasn't Allyson.

"She's not waving at the crowds, either," Stephie said.

"She was okay a few minutes ago," I said. "Maybe she's just tired. She was really sick with the flu a couple of weeks ago."

I watched her more closely as she rode along. She usually had great posture and a pretty smile. Now her shoulders were slumped and her head was bent strangely. I rode up beside her. She didn't even look up until I called her name.

"Allyson, are you okay?" I asked her.

She turned her head toward me as if it took a lot of effort. Her face looked flushed like she had a fever.

"I'm fine," she said. "Just really tired."

"Why don't you drop out of the parade?" I asked. "I'll come with you."

"No way. This is your first parade, Kell. Enjoy it." She smiled and waved to a group of kids. "I'll be okay. Really."

"Okay," I said. I dropped back to ride beside my friends. "Allyson says she's fine," I assured them.

Brian shrugged. "Okay. Hey, did you know

9

that teenagers are 50 percent more likely to catch a cold than people over fifty?"

"Yeah," I said, "and men are twice as likely to get leprosy as women."

Stephie shook her head in mock disgust. "You two are nuts."

Brian winked at me. "Sure, but we're so funny," he said.

Brian moved to the row behind us. Stephie chattered on about the parade and our upcoming barrel race team tryouts. I'd picked Western-style riding and barrel racing because I could do them better than Allyson. Making the team and winning in my age group would be even more exciting than being in the parade. Well, maybe.

When we reached the end of the parade route, I saw Mom and Dad waving wildly. This had been one of the best days of my life. I was sorry it was over.

Everybody started loading their horses into trailers. "I'll see you guys back at the center," Brian called.

I wasn't sure if he was talking to Allyson or to Stephie and me, but I yelled back to him. "How about some barrel racing later today? Allyson is coming, too."

He didn't answer me. I guess all the horses snorting and the kids yelling were too loud.

Just as I was about to call to him again, Ally pulled me aside.

"Kelly, I don't think I can make it to the barrel racing after the parade."

"What's wrong? Are you feeling worse?"

"I'm just really tired. I'll be okay. I think I need to rest for a little while," she said.

Ally was trying to make it sound like nothing, but I didn't like the way she looked. An uneasy feeling settled in my stomach. A breeze rustled my hair. Suddenly, I felt cold.

*   *   *   *   *

I stayed at the equestrian center to work out. When I got home, I found a note saying Mom and Dad had gone to the office. I figured Allyson was feeling better and had gone out with her friends. But as I passed her room, I saw her lying on her bed. She was staring at the ceiling. She still wore her boots and riding clothes.

"Ally?" I tapped on the open door.

She rose up on her elbow. "Oh, hi, Kell."

"You okay?" I asked.

"Sure. I'm just resting." She dropped back down on the pillows. "I guess I've been doing too much lately." She sounded out of breath.

"You're sure that's all it is?" I asked.

11

Allyson usually had enough energy for six people. She's the kind of person who loves life and wants to experience everything.

"I'm fine," she snapped back. That wasn't like her either.

Don't get me wrong. Ally isn't a saint or anything. But she is really nice and almost everybody likes her. She taught me how to dance, how to put on makeup, and how to talk to guys. The one thing we don't talk about, though, is Brian. I don't have the courage to tell her how I feel about him—especially since I think he likes her.

I looked around her room. You wouldn't think somebody who's only seventeen could have won so many prizes and ribbons and trophies. My favorite was a medal she'd won in her very first competition. Dad had had it mounted on black velvet in a shadow box frame. Maybe I'd win a big competition someday and make everybody proud of me, too.

I turned back to Allyson. She was all curled up, her knees pulled up to her chest.

"Wouldn't you sleep better if you got out of those clothes?" I asked. "I'll help you."

"It's not necess—" She stopped, then sighed. She straightened out. "Thanks," she said as if that little bit of movement was too much for her.

As I helped her take off the boots and riding clothes, I noticed that her ankles and stomach were swollen. Her skin felt hot. I was worried about her, but I pretended that I didn't notice. I didn't want her to know that I was a little scared.

"When are Mom and Dad coming home?" I asked casually.

"By dinner time. They're bringing pizza," she said.

"I hope it's got lots of anchovies and—"

Allyson's hand flew to her mouth. She groaned. "Stop! Please don't mention food."

"I'm sorry, Ally. Boy, you *must* be sick. Uh, I'm going to go call Mom and Dad at the office," I said.

I thought she'd say no, but instead she nodded. "Kelly, something's wrong with me. I've never felt like this with the flu."

"What do you think it is?" I asked her.

"I don't know. Look how swollen I am. Kelly, I'm scared. When I went to the bathroom, my urine looked dark."

Suddenly, she jumped off the bed and ran to the bathroom. I heard her vomiting.

I rushed to the phone and punched the office number. *Be there. Please be there!*

Finally my dad answered, "Reeds' Agency."

"Dad! Come home quick. Ally's sick!"

Two

"MOM, is Ally going to be all right?" I asked for about the tenth time. Mom and Dad had come right home when I called and we took Ally to the hospital. It felt as if we'd been in the emergency room for a year. "How much longer do we have to wait?"

"Until the doctors finish examining her," Mom said. "Why don't you go outside and get some fresh air?"

An ambulance siren wailed in the distance. "I'd rather stay here," I said.

"Honey, it might be a long time yet. I'll come and get you," Mom promised.

The emergency waiting room was full of people with sprains and breaks and assorted minor injuries. The closed-circuit TV was demonstrating how to do the Heimlich maneuver to help someone who was choking. I'd watched it at least four times already.

14

I got up and walked around, wishing I could get a glimpse of Allyson in one of the little emergency cubicles. What were they doing to my sister? She couldn't be really sick. She couldn't die or anything, could she? I pushed that thought out of my mind. She was going to be okay. She had to be.

I walked outside to a little patio and sat on the cement edge that surrounded a fountain. A spray of water, blown by the breeze, cooled my face.

I closed my eyes and pictured Allyson and Airborne jumping fences together, flying through the air as if they were one. I remembered Allyson, looking beautiful in white and silver, winning the Miss Teen Contest. I could see her being named Homecoming Queen and skiing down a slope at Snow Valley. I sighed. Nothing bad could happen to someone who was so happy, so full of life. Could it?

"Kelly?"

The sound of my dad's voice brought me out of my thoughts.

"Come on in now," he said from the entranceway to the hospital.

"Is Allyson done?" I asked, looking around. "Where's Mom and the doctor?"

"We've already talked to him," Dad said. "Your mother's in with Allyson."

"Mom promised to come get me," I said.

"I'm sorry, Kelly," Dad said. He put his arm around me and gave my shoulders a little squeeze. "The doctor had another emergency. He only had a minute to talk with us."

"What did he say? What's wrong with her? Allyson just has the flu, right? She's going to be okay, isn't she?" I asked.

He led me over to a couch. He sat beside me and took my hand. "She's all right for the moment, so try not to worry," Dad said. He's always so calm about everything, but his voice sounded strained. "The hospital is making arrangements to give her a room."

"Hospital? Dad, please tell me what's wrong with her."

"Allyson has kidney failure," Dad said gently. "Her kidneys can no longer remove the waste products from her body. They have to do more tests to see if it's chronic. That means her condition can't be reversed."

Kidney failure. A knot of fear twisted my stomach. "Is she going to—to die?" I asked.

"We don't know yet how serious it is," Dad said, his voice breaking slightly. "Her condition is worse right now because she also has the flu."

"Did the flu cause it?" I asked. "Is that why she was puffy and got sick and everything?"

16

"They don't know for sure what caused it," Dad said. "The doctor thinks she may have a kidney disease with a long technical name. They are going to do a biopsy on her. That means they're going to take a sample of the tissue and examine—"

"I know what a biopsy is, Dad."

"She has to go on hemodialysis," he continued. "A machine will have to take over the work of her kidneys."

Kidney failure. Allyson hooked up to a machine?

"Our lives are going to be changed," Dad said, looking down at the floor. "We'll be counting on you to help out, honey."

"You know I'll do anything for Ally."

He nodded and gave my hand a squeeze. I had never seen my dad looking so, well, so scared. "I just wanted to warn you that it's not going to be easy for—" He stopped as Mom walked toward us.

"How's Allyson doing?" Dad asked.

"She's scared," Mom said, "but she's trying to pretend like nothing's wrong at all."

"Can I see her?" I asked.

"Not until she's in a room." Mom let out a deep sigh. She looked bad, too. "We might as well go down to the cafeteria," she went on, "while we're waiting."

"How can anybody even think about food now?" I asked.

Mom touched my cheek and looked at me as if she were afraid something was going to happen to me, too. "We have to keep up our strength," she said softly.

We headed for the elevators. As we took a crowded elevator down to the cafeteria, I felt as if I was in a cage and it was closing in around me. *Allyson's going to be all right. She's going to be all right.* I kept saying that over and over to myself.

The cafeteria was almost empty. The line of plastic-covered sandwiches and salads didn't look appetizing. "I'm not hungry," I said, even though it was long past supper time.

"Try to eat something," Mom urged.

I chose a ham and cheese sandwich. I nibbled at it, but it felt like a chunk of concrete in my stomach. Mom picked at her salad. Dad stirred three spoonfuls of sugar into his coffee, then kept stirring and stirring until I wanted to scream. I'd never seen them look so worried. It scared me. *Please let Ally be all right,* I pleaded silently.

* * * * *

Visiting hours were almost over by the time we got to see Allyson. She had a room on the third floor. I saw a sign that said no one under fourteen could go above the first floor. I was glad I'd had my fourteenth birthday last month.

As we walked down the corridor, I glanced in the rooms, wondering what was wrong with each person. I thought about how great it must be to be a doctor and help all these people. I just hoped the doctors could help Ally.

Allyson was lying still in her bed. There were tubes hooked up to a gross-looking machine with flashing lights. I could actually see her blood in a plastic thing about the size of a flashlight.

She tried to sit up, but I could see how weak she was.

"Honey, you lie still," Mom told her.

"I'm okay," Allyson said.

I went over to the bed. "Boy, you sure scared me," I said.

"It's nothing to get upset over, Kell. I'll be out of here in no time. The doctor said my kidneys weren't working. It's nothing," Allyson said.

I glanced at Mom. Allyson never liked to admit that anything was wrong with her. But Ally must have known how serious kidney failure was. Mom and Dad fussed around Allyson. I really felt sorry for her. If she had to be on this machine for the rest of her life, I didn't think she could cope with it.

"Hey, Sis, you look like you're part of a video game," I joked, so Ally wouldn't know how worried I was about her.

She gave me a weak smile.

"How long do you have to be on this thing?" I asked.

"Two or three days a week," she said glumly. "I'm going to be stuck on this—this thing several hours at a time."

Allyson is definitely not a good patient. I could imagine her trying to walk down the halls, dragging the machine behind her. When we were younger and she had broken her leg, I caught her trying to cut off the fiberglass cast. She just doesn't like to be confined.

The nurse came in then and said Allyson needed to rest.

Mom and Dad kissed Allyson. I gave her a hug and whispered, "If there's anything I can do, tell me."

"There is something I'd like you to do. Call Keith and tell him I can't go to the movies with him tomorrow night," she said. "But don't tell him I'm in the hospital."

"Why not?" I asked. She'd been going with

him for over a year. "Don't you want him to visit you?"

"No!" she answered. "Don't tell anybody about this."

"So, what am I supposed to say?" I asked, teasing her. "That you've gone to Disneyland?"

"Tell everybody I have the flu and I don't want to pass it on to anyone else." She sat up again. "Promise?"

"Sure, but if I ever go to the hospital, I want tons of flowers and cards."

As we left, Allyson said brightly, "Don't look so worried, all of you. I'm fine."

If it made her feel better to pretend nothing was wrong, that was okay with me. I just wished it was true.

* * * * *

When I came home from school a few days later, I hurried to Allyson's room. Mom had brought her home from the hospital that morning. Allyson sat at her dresser, carefully examining her face in the mirror.

"You look gorgeous, Ally." I rushed over to her and gave her a hug. "I'm glad you're home. Boy, have I missed you."

I looked at her carefully. There wasn't any puffiness in her face and there weren't any

21

dark circles beneath her eyes.

"The swelling's gone," I told her. "You look terrific."

"I don't know," she said doubtfully. "Do you think anybody will know I've been in the hospital?"

"You mean you aren't going to tell Keith—ever?" I asked.

"No, at least not now," Allyson said. "He hates sickness stuff. His grandmother lived with his family when she was dying of cancer. No way am I going to tell him about me."

I sat down on her bed. "Isn't he going to get kind of curious when you disappear all the time for treatments?"

Allyson's face turned pink with anger. "I asked the doctor to talk to Mom about another method. It's called peritoneal dialysis. They implant a tube into your stomach. All the blood is cleansed inside the body."

"That would be great," I said. "You wouldn't be stuck on a machine."

"Right. I could go everywhere and not feel like a dog on a leash," she said.

The doctor had given us some pamphlets. I'd read all about dialysis and kidney disease.

"That peritoneal method isn't all that simple," I said, trying to sound like an expert. "You have to keep everything sterile."

"I know. When the doctor said there was a chance of getting peritonitis, Mom looked nervous about it. But I want to try it," Allyson said.

Mom probably didn't trust Allyson to do the procedure right or on time. She'd get so busy with all her activities that she'd forget to do it.

"The doctor said the only other treatment is a transplant. But I don't know if I could do that. Unless a family member gives up a kidney, it can take years before you can get one that matches your own blood and tissue type."

"How about me? I'll give you one of mine," I offered eagerly.

"Don't be silly, Kell. You're too young. You have to be eighteen to do it. Anyway, I don't even want to think about a transplant. Maybe the dialysis will make me okay," she said.

But a few days after that, when we got the test results, they weren't very promising. They showed that Ally did have a chronic condition that couldn't be cured. I felt so sorry for her. Her whole life was going to change now. And I knew ours would, too.

"So, when do you go for your next treatment?" I asked.

"I have to go three times a week to a dialysis

center, but only until we get one of the machines."

"Really? You'll have one of those weird machines right here in the house?"

She nodded.

"How soon?" I asked.

"We have to have special plumbing and a water treatment system put in," Allyson explained. "Mom and I have to take a six-week training course to learn how to use the machine." Tears welled up in Allyson's eyes. "And I have to have a permanent graft put in my arm so an artery and a vein can be hooked up to the machine."

Then Allyson looked down and I saw the tears rolling down her cheeks. "Oh, Kelly, I hate all of this. I hate it!"

"It'll be easier at home," I said, trying to make her feel better. I put my arm around her. "I'm sorry, Ally. I'll help any way I can. I'll bet it won't be so bad once you get used to it."

"I'll never get used to it. I can't eat what I want. I can't even drink when I'm thirsty. I can't even go to the bathroom anymore. I can't do anything. Nothing will ever be the same again," she said and broke out in sobs.

Three

SINCE Ally had gotten sick a couple of weeks before, I kept away from Stephie as much as I could. It was hard for me to see my friends or Ally's friends and not tell them what was happening. I couldn't understand why Allyson wouldn't let me tell anybody about her kidneys. To me, it seemed like she needed her friends more than ever. But I'd made a promise to her, so I kept quiet.

When the telephone rang that night during supper, I knew it was Stephie. She was probably wondering why I'd been avoiding her. I jumped up from the table.

"I'll get it," I said and hurried into the study for more privacy.

"What's going on?" Stephie asked before I could get a word in. "You didn't show up at the equestrian center yesterday. You rush out of class. Are you mad at me or something?"

"I can't talk about it now," I whispered.

"Want to meet me at the library in 15 minutes?"

"Sure," she whispered back. Allyson might not want to tell Keith, but I just couldn't keep secrets from my best friend. I hurried back to the table and gobbled down the rest of my spaghetti and salad. "Can I go to the library?" I asked. "Stephie and I have to study for a test."

That was true. Ever since Allyson got sick, I hadn't been able to concentrate on my school work.

"All right," Mom said absently. She was busy watching that Allyson didn't drink too much iced tea.

"I'll be home by nine," I said, but I doubted that anybody was listening.

Steph was waiting for me on the library steps. "Okay, okay, tell me what's going on," she said. "You sounded so mysterious on the phone."

"You have to swear you won't tell anybody—and I mean it," I told her.

She crossed her heart. "I promise. You can trust me."

"It's Allyson," I told her. Some kids passed us and I whispered, "Wait. Let's go where no one will hear us." We headed out to the rose garden in back of the library and sat on a bench.

"What about your sister?" Steph asked.

"She's been in the hospital." I told Steph about rushing Allyson to the emergency room. "She has something called RPGN—Rapid Progressive Glomerulonephritis."

"Only *you* would remember a word like that," she said. "What's it mean?"

"Her kidneys don't work anymore," I explained. "She has to be on a kidney machine for the rest of her life."

"That's awful, Kelly, but why the big secret? Lots of people have kidney problems, don't they?"

"Yeah. I read in one of the pamphlets that over 30,000 people develop kidney failure every year. But that doesn't make it any easier when you're one of those people," I said. "And Ally feels weird about it."

"No wonder you've been acting strange lately," she said. "Thanks for telling me."

"You can't tell anybody. Allyson doesn't want Keith or anyone to know she has to be on dialysis. Okay?" I asked.

"I promised," Steph said. "What's dialysis? Is it some kind of medicine?"

"No," I said. "It's an artificial kidney machine that cleanses the blood."

"It must be rough. Is she going to be able to ride horses anymore?" Steph asked.

"I don't know yet. She and Mom have to go

through a training program. They'll learn about it," I explained. "Anyway, that's why I haven't seen you lately."

"How about going to the center tomorrow after school?" Stephie asked. "We need to practice for the barrel races."

"I don't know if I can," I said, torn between wanting to practice and being with Allyson. "I might have to help Ally. I want to learn all about dialysis, too."

"Okay. Just don't forget we have that big competition coming up in October," Steph reminded me.

"How could I forget? You know how badly I want to make the team," I said. Until Allyson got sick, I'd been getting up at 4:30 three times a week to work out with Sidekick at the center. I'd just about die if I didn't make the team. Maybe I'd win a medal and Dad would get it framed in a fancy shadow box, like he did for Ally's award.

"I really want to make the team. But helping my sister is more important than any competition," I said, "even though sometimes I'm not sure if anyone notices I'm helping."

"Kel, do you feel left out of things at home?" Steph asked me.

"Oh, I don't know," I said with a shrug. I felt kind of selfish complaining about it. "Mom and Dad can't help it if they're busy with

Allyson and their work and everything."

"Ever since Jonathan was born, all Mom and Dad talk about is how cute and wonderful he is. Nobody pays attention to me or what I do anymore," Steph said. "It makes me mad sometimes."

"They don't mean to ignore me," I said in my family's defense. Then I sighed and decided to tell her more. "I feel so bad for Ally, but sometimes I want to shake them and say I'm here, too. It's like I could leave for a day and nobody would notice."

That's what's so great about being best friends with Steph. We can tell each other our deep down feelings.

"You're luckier than I am," Steph said. "Allyson's seventeen. She'll be leaving home pretty soon. Jonathan's only a year old." She grinned. "I have to put up with him for years." Her smile faded. "But even if Jonathan is a pain sometimes, I couldn't stand it if he got sick."

We talked a little while longer, then went into the library to study. We're both taking an advanced math class, and it's really hard. I like science and biology better—any courses that will help me become a doctor someday.

As we headed toward our usual spot, Steph nudged me. "Hey, look. There's Brian."

He was studying with his friend Rob

Donello. Steph thinks Rob is cute, but I think he's a jerk. All he ever talks about are sports and his new video games. And he's not as good looking as Brian is. Brian is tall and blond with blue-gray eyes. Rob is shorter and muscular, like a wrestler.

Brian looked up, grinned, and motioned for us to come over to their table.

"Are you going to tell Brian about your sister?" Stephie whispered.

"No. And don't forget your promise," I reminded her. "You know what a bigmouth Rob is."

Before I could even set my notebook on the table, Rob asked, "So what's wrong with Allyson?"

"W-what are you talking about?" I stammered.

"I heard she was in the hospital," he said.

"Where did you hear that?" I asked. How could anyone have known that?

"My aunt is a volunteer at the hospital. She saw your sister there."

I didn't know what to say. I'd promised Allyson not to tell anybody.

Brian glared at Rob. "How come you never told me, Rob? Kelly, is she okay? Was she in an accident? What?"

"She's going to be fine," I said. "She, uhh, just has a little kidney problem." I had to tell them something. I couldn't just ignore them and walk away. Then who knew what kind of rumors they'd spread around school?

"That's not what I heard," Rob said in a hushed voice. "I heard she has leukemia. I'm really sor—"

"I don't know where you got *that* information," I said angrily. "That's not true at all."

Rob shrugged. "I hope you're right."

"Well, I ought to know. She's *my* sister. And you better not go around and spread lies about her," I warned him.

The librarian walked over to the table. "Is everything all right here?"

"We're just studying," Brian said quickly. "We'll try to be quieter."

As soon as the librarian left, Brian whispered, "I'm sure glad Allyson is okay."

I nodded and gathered up my stuff. I didn't feel like studying anymore. "I have to go," I said and started walking.

"Want me to come with you?" Stephie asked.

I shook my head. "No. But thanks, though. See you guys tomorrow."

I hurried outside and ran toward home.

Poor Allyson. It was bad enough that she had to deal with kidney failure. How would she cope with the idea that everyone thought she had leukemia?

* * * * *

Allyson met me at the door. "Why are you watching for me?" I asked. "Don't tell me you're worried about my being out after dark."

"You promised!" Ally yelled. She hardly ever got angry, but she sounded furious. "I asked you not to tell anyone that I was sick."

"I didn't tell—" I stopped. I had told Steph.

"Mrs. Miller just called Mom to offer her help. She said she was so sorry I was ill. You just had to tell Steph, didn't you?"

Mom interrupted before I could answer. "The least you could do is to respect your sister's wishes," she said to me.

"I did tell Steph just now, but she didn't have time to talk to her mom. She was still at the library when I left. Anyway, Rob Donello said he heard that you have leukemia."

"Leukemia?" Mom and Dad said at the same time. "Stephanie's mother never said anything about that."

Allyson's face turned white. Her mouth kept opening and closing, but no words came out.

"Take it easy," I said. "It's okay. I told my friends you just had a little kidney problem. It's better they know the truth than think you're dying of cancer, isn't it?"

32

"Keith." She choked out the word. "I didn't want him to know. He'll avoid me now for sure."

"Allyson, honey, everything will—" Mom began.

"I don't want to talk about it!" Ally yelled and headed toward her bedroom.

I ran after her. "Wait up, Ally."

"Leave me alone. All of you, just leave me alone!"

Tears stung my eyes. My sister hardly ever spoke to anybody that way—and never to me.

Mom put her arm around me. "She doesn't mean it, honey. She's angry and hurt and has to take it out on someone."

I nodded, but how could a disease change someone as sweet and caring as Allyson? I hated her disease, too. I almost wished I could change places with her.

A few minutes later she slammed out of her room. "I'm going out," she informed Mom and Dad. She had a look on her face that said, *Don't try to stop me.*

I heard her take off in her car, tires squealing. Mom looked at Dad. "We should've stopped her," Mom said, almost in tears.

"Allyson's always been responsible," Dad said. "She needs to let off steam."

"Kelly, don't you have homework?" Mom asked, her voice sharp. "Go do it right now."

"I've done it."

"Don't argue with me, young lady. Do as I say."

"Well, pardon me for living," I muttered under my breath. Just because Allyson ran off. they didn't need to take it out on me.

I ran to my room and flung myself on the bed. *I wish I were old enough to drive*, I thought. *I'd take off, too. Nobody around here would care.*

A few minutes later there was a light tap on the door. "Kelly? May I come in?" Mom asked.

I switched on my bedside lamp. "I guess so."

Mom came over to the bed and sat beside me. "Sweetheart, I'm sorry I snapped at you."

"That's okay," I mumbled.

"No, it isn't. I'm just so worried about Allyson, that I forget you're having a rough time, too." I didn't say anything and she took my hand. "You know that your father and I love you just as much as we do Allyson, don't you?"

"It sure doesn't seem like it," I said.

"I know, honey. But right now she needs our attention." She gave a little laugh. "I'll tell you something, though. Sometimes, I forget that you're only fourteen. Maybe your father and I don't say it often enough, but we're very proud of you, Kelly."

"Honest? Even though I don't have lots of trophies like Ally does?"

She gave me a hug. "You get the blue ribbon for being the best daughter in your age group." She walked over to the window and looked out at the wet streets. I knew she was worried about Ally.

"She's a good driver, Mom," I said. "She'll be okay."

"I hope so. Oh, I hope so."

She kissed me goodnight. "Try to get some sleep now," she said. "And remember that your dad and I love you."

"I love you, too."

After Mom left, I got undressed. Warmed by her words, I hardly noticed the cold. I snuggled down in bed, feeling a little better about things. I think I fell asleep the minute my head hit the pillow.

I was jolted awake by the overhead light. "Kelly!"

I sat bolt upright, wide awake. Allyson was standing beside my bed. "Kell—I'm sick..." She sounded as if she was having trouble breathing.

"Lie down," I told her. "I'll get Mom and Dad."

"I don't want to bother them. Oh, Kell, I was so stupid!"

"You didn't have an accident with the car?"

She shook her head. "I went to the drive-in and drank five large colas, one after the other."

"Ally, you didn't! You're only allowed four cups in a whole day."

"I don't know what got into me." She tried to smile. "Besides a gallon or so of soda."

"You must feel like you're going to explode," I said.

She groaned. "I do and it's my own fault."

"I'm going to get Mom." Before she could argue, I hurried down the long hall to their bedroom. "Mom, Dad, hurry. Ally's sick."

Mom and Dad took her to the emergency room. Ally had to go on dialysis to get rid of all the liquid she'd drunk. Luckily, she was going to be okay.

I hadn't really thought how awful it must be not to be able to do normal things. I took lots of things for granted, things like going to the bathroom. No wonder Allyson felt so frustrated and angry.

I promised myself I'd try not to get upset when she snapped at me. I knew she was going through a lot. Now it looked like it was my turn to be the big sister for her. I wasn't sure I could do it.

Four

THE next few weeks were hectic. I skipped a lot of my early morning workouts at the equestrian center because I was too sleepy. Allyson tried to act like she didn't want me hanging around. But I figured that it must make her feel good to know that I cared so much about her.

Ally never talked about it, but I knew she was hurt because Keith had never called her. I didn't know for sure if the news had gotten to him, though the odds were pretty good that it had. Ally had trouble sleeping, so we'd sit up watching the late shows on TV.

Her beautiful yellow-and-white bedroom looked more like a hospital room. The special plumbing for her dialysis machine had been installed. The "monster" and all the supplies were everywhere. Boxes around the room contained two gallon jugs of dialysate to cleanse her blood, rubber gloves, forceps, plastic tubes, and big, thick needles.

Mom fixed up an office in the study so she could work part of the time at home. I had begged to take the six-week course with Mom and Allyson. But Dad felt I was too young to be trusted with something as important as dialysis.

Until Mom and Allyson learned how to use the machine, Allyson had to travel 20 miles to the closest dialysis center for her treatments. At breakfast on one of Allyson's treatment days, I asked Mom if I could go along. I'd asked before and always got a big fat no as the answer.

"Please, Mom. Just this once," I pleaded.

"I don't know why you'd want to go there," Allyson said, sounding irritated.

Mom nodded. "It's no place for young people. Anyway, you'd just be in the way."

"Nobody cares around here that I want to be a doctor. And, besides, Ally is my sister. I have a right to be there, too—"

Allyson threw her hands in the air. "Stop arguing, you two! Let her come if she wants." Allyson ran from the room.

"What's wrong with her?" I asked. "I was telling her that I care about her." When Mom didn't say anything, I went on. "Ally isn't like herself anymore at all. Nobody can say a word without her blowing up."

"She's going through a hard time right now," Mom said softly. "She's used to being able to eat anything she wants and to do anything she wants. She resents it that her body has betrayed her. Just try to be patient with her."

"I am, but sometimes it's hard, you know. I wish she'd get back to being like herself again."

Mom let out a deep sigh and I realized how tired she looked. "So do I," she whispered.

"It's okay if I go with you today?"

"Oh, I suppose." She gave me a weak smile. "I wish you were old enough to drive."

"Why can't Allyson and I go while you get some rest? She can drive."

"I can't let you two go there alone," Mom said. "I just can't do it."

*   *   *   *   *

Allyson was probably the youngest person at the dialysis center. Little kids had to go to a special pediatric unit. The center was actually kind of neat inside. There were 10 recliners on each side of a long room. People were reading or watching the TVs above each chair. Everybody was friendly and seemed to know each other. It was kind of like a club.

Mom went to do some errands while Allyson got dialysized. I sat on a stool next to Allyson's chair. She kept her eyes closed so she couldn't see what was going on, but I watched closely as the nurse hooked a tube to Allyson's chest.

A woman in a recliner next to Allyson was celebrating her thirtieth birthday. The staff had brought in special foods to help her celebrate.

"Is this your first time?" she asked Allyson. "I haven't seen you here before."

"I've been coming for a few weeks now," Allyson said. "How long have you been on dialysis?"

"I had a transplant recently but my body rejected it, so I'm back here again for treatments," the woman replied.

"Oh, that's awful," Allyson said. "You must be really disappointed."

"I thought they had new drugs now that kept the body from rejecting the kidney," I spoke up.

"They do, but I guess I was too busy. I kept forgetting to take my medicine."

I was thinking how stupid that was and I guess she could tell from the look on my face.

"You try running after two hyperactive little kids," she said quickly. "Anyway, I don't mind coming here three times a week. It's a wonderful place." She gave a little laugh. "And it's the only rest I get."

While Allyson was on the machine, a dietician came to talk to her about the need to follow a strict diet. She couldn't eat too many fruits, vegetables, dairy products, or fast foods. And she was permitted only a certain amount of liquid each day. I sure didn't envy her. I'd really miss pizzas and pop and peanuts—all my favorite foods. I tried to joke about it.

"You're lucky, Ally. You can't eat a lot of stuff, but you also can't eat broccoli and spinach," I said.

"Yeah, I'm lucky, all right. I can't go out for hamburgers or pizzas with my friends."

"That's not true," the dietician told her. "You just have to be careful. You can ask the waitress to fix your hamburger without salt, tomatoes, or pickles. Just take a tiny piece of pizza without sausage or peppers."

"I don't want to ask for special things. I hate feeling different from all my friends," Ally complained.

"It's perfectly normal to feel angry about this at first," the dietician said. "It'll take time to get used to it. One of the most important things, though, is to talk about your feelings with your family and friends."

"I can't," Allyson said. "Nobody understands."

"I do," I said quickly. "You can talk to me. You can wake me up any time, even in the middle of the night. I'll stay home from school to talk."

Allyson smiled, and she looked more like her old self. "You're such a nut, Kelly, but I love you."

I smiled back at her. I wouldn't trade those words for anything in the world.

"If you don't mind," Allyson said to us, "I'd like to rest. I didn't get much sleep last night."

"There's a lounge where you can watch TV or read," the dietician said to me.

"Do you think I could look around?" I asked. "I want to be a doctor. I promise I won't get in the way."

She arranged for me to get a tour. I got to see where they sterilized the artificial kidneys. It was all done with computers. I saw the big vats of dialysate, saline, and even vinegar. The contamination room held the huge containers where all the wastes were put to be picked up and taken to a special site.

While I waited in the lounge, I sat next to a guy who looked about twenty-five.

"Hi," I said and smiled. "Are you waiting for somebody on dialysis, too?"

"No, I just finished my treatment. I'm waiting for my mom. She won't let me drive home," he explained.

"I know what you mean. My sister's on dialysis and my mother treats her like she's going to break or something."

"I guess mothers are like that," he said.

We started talking. I learned his name was Tom. He was cute for an older guy. I noticed that he was wearing a beeper.

"Are you a doctor or something?" I asked. He touched the beeper and smiled.

"No. Nobody in my family was a good match for a kidney transplant, so I've been waiting for one from someone who's died. I've been on the waiting list for over a year."

That reminded me of the woman getting dialysis beside Ally. He'd probably be mad at her if he heard that she was too busy to take care of her new kidney.

"A kidney might be available at any time of the day or night," Tom said. "I even have a bag packed so I can get to the hospital in a hurry whenever a kidney is available from an accident vict—" He stopped. "I guess that must sound terrible to you."

"No. I think it's great. I'll bet it helps the family to know something good can come from something sad like an accident," I said. "And, besides, you don't cause the accident."

"A computer has the names and blood and tissue types of all of us that need kidneys. There are nearly 8,500 people waiting."

"You must go nuts waiting for that beeper to go off," I said.

"Yeah," he said with a laugh. "I keep checking the batteries to be sure it's working. At first, I kept bugging the nurses to tell me how long I'd have to wait. But they have no way of knowing."

"Kelly?" Allyson called from the door to the lounge. "It's time to go."

"Come and meet Tom," I said. "He's—"

She gave him a smile that just barely moved her lips. "I'm sorry, but Mom's waiting in the car." She abruptly walked away.

"I'm sorry, Tom. My sister didn't used to be like that."

"I know exactly what she's going through," he said. "It'll get easier."

"Yeah, I hope so. Bye," I said as I left. "I hope your beeper goes off really soon."

* * * * *

One day I got home from school earlier than usual. I found a note from Mom saying she was out grocery shopping. I could hear Allyson's radio playing.

I grabbed something to eat before I went in to see how she was doing. The phone rang in her room. Her friends, all except Keith, kept calling to see how she was doing, but she refused to see any of them. The phone rang and rang. At first, I was irritated that Ally

44

wouldn't answer it. But then it occurred to me that something might be wrong with her. She might be sick again.

I dropped my sandwich and rushed into her room. Ally was sitting on her bedroom floor. She was going through her scrapbooks. And right next to all her prized memories was a huge bowl filled with potato chips. She was stuffing them into her mouth one by one. I ran to grab the phone.

"Leave it alone!" she said angrily, trying to hide the crackly potato chip bag behind her back. "I don't want to talk to anybody."

I just stared at her until the phone stopped ringing. She was still in her nightgown and she hadn't even brushed her hair.

"Didn't you go to school today? What's wrong?" I asked her.

"Nothing," she muttered. "I just didn't feel like going today, that's all."

"Weren't they going to choose the debate team today?"

"Drop it, Kelly."

She'd won first place last year. I knew she'd wanted to make the team again.

"May I have some chips, too?" I asked, changing the subject.

She tossed the bag at me. "Go ahead. Say it. 'Allyson, you know you're not supposed to eat salty things,'" she said, mimicking Mom.

"I know it must be hard to stay on your diet." I sat down on the floor beside her. "Don't you feel worse when you eat the wrong—"

"Look at this picture," she said, cutting me off. "Remember when Airborne and I won our first ribbon?"

"Yep. I was only seven, but I knew I wanted to have a horse and ride just like you," I said.

She reached over and tousled my hair. "You're funny the way you always try to copy me." Then her smile faded. "Are you going to get sick, too?" she asked softly.

"I'm sorry, Ally. I wish there was something I could do to make things easier for you," I said and meant it.

"No, I'm the one who's sorry. It's not your fault that I'm sick and feel crummy and tired all the time." She put her arm around me and gave me a quick hug. "I know I've been acting rotten lately, but I can't seem to stop it."

"It's okay, Ally."

"Kelly, I feel so—so helpless, so dependent on that stupid machine." Ally nodded toward the monster that she would start using next week.

"You remember that guy Tom at the dialysis center?" I asked.

She nodded. "I saw him there before. What about him?"

46

"He's waiting for a kidney transplant. Wouldn't that be a lot easier than being on dialysis?" I asked.

"Maybe. The doctor has talked to me about it, but I don't like the idea of an operation." Ally pulled up her long sleeve and looked down at the permanent graft on her red, swollen arm. "This is bad enough."

"You ought to at least think about it," I said.

"I'll think about it," Ally said.

"Maybe it would help if—" I hesitated, not wanting to upset her even more.

"I know what you're going to say. You think I should start doing things again."

"The doctor said you should exercise," I reminded her. "He said you could do almost everything if you're careful." I got on my knees and said excitedly, "Ally, let's go riding tomorrow. Just the two of us."

She shook her head. "No. You and Stephie are getting ready for the barrel race competition, aren't you?"

"Yes, but that's not important," I lied. "I'd rather be with you."

"Of course it's important, Kelly Belly." We both smiled at the name she used to call me when I was a chubby four-year-old. "This is your first big competition coming up."

"I just wish there was something I could do to make you feel better."

47

"There is," she said with a crooked smile. "Take those potato chips out of here."

"I'm going to ask Mom not to buy that kind of stuff anymore," I said. I grabbed up the bag. "Whatever you can't eat, I won't eat either."

"You're weird, you know that?" She grinned the first real smile I'd seen in weeks. "Weird or not, I wouldn't trade you for any other sister in the world."

"Me, either," I said. Now that she was in a good mood, I brought up a subject she kept avoiding. "Let me call Keith and tell him— "

"No! I don't want you begging him to come and see me," she snapped.

"Okay, okay, but I still think you should talk to him."

"Well, how are you two?" Mom asked from the doorway. "Allyson, I bought you—" She stopped in midsentence and frowned at me. "Kelly Annabel Reed! How could you?"

"How could I what?" I stumbled over the words, frantically trying to think what I'd done wrong.

"You know your sister loves potato chips. I can't believe you'd be so cruel and insensitive as to eat them in front of Allyson."

I glanced down at the bag of chips in my hand, then turned and winked at Allyson. "I'm sorry, Sis. You'll never find another bag of chips in this room."

"Kelly, come and help me put away the groceries," Mom said.

"I'll get dressed and help, too," Allyson said.

"No, it's not fair for you to have to look at all the food you can't have," Mom told her. "I bought some special things for you. They'll make it easier for you to stay on your diet."

I noticed Allyson's shoulders slump. I knew she hated being treated as if she were different from everybody else, like she wasn't part of the family anymore.

"The doctor and the social worker said she should try to live a normal life," I said. "Maybe she'd feel better if she did some things around the house."

"Kelly, it won't hurt you to do Allyson's chores for a while longer," Mom said, completely missing the point.

"I'm not trying to get out of work. I just think—"

"You think too much," Mom said.

Knowing Mom, there was no point in arguing. On my way to the kitchen, I crumpled the bag and stuffed it deep into the garbage can. I knew Mom and Dad would go right on treating Allyson like an invalid. I hated it, but who would listen to what I had to say?

Five

I woke up early the next morning feeling rest-less. I was a little nervous about the time trials for the barrel races. I buttoned my shirt wrong and put on two socks that didn't match. Even though I tried not to think too much about it, I did want to be on the team more than almost anything in the world.

At breakfast I managed to drink a glass of juice. I was too nervous—and scared—to eat. I knew I hadn't practiced enough the last few weeks. I was worried. What if I didn't make the team?

Mom was still wearing her robe. Dad was eating some toast. Allyson never joined us for breakfast anymore.

"You're coming to the center to watch today, aren't you?" I asked them.

"I have to show a two million-dollar house this morning," Dad said. "I'm sorry I can't be there, but this could be a big deal for all of us."

I guess he saw how disappointed I looked because he added, "I should be able to help you out next week. We'll get you ready for that competition."

"Thanks, Dad," I said. With his help I'd be sure to win in Sacramento. "How about you, Mom?"

"I'm sorry, honey. Allyson and I have our last class on using the dialysis machine," Mom said. "It's pretty complicated."

Just like a balloon, my family popped some of the excitement right out of my day. You would think that somebody in my family would care enough to come and watch me.

I was still grumbling to myself when I met Steph and Brian in the tackroom at the equestrian center. "Hi, you two," I said. "Are you guys nervous?"

"Are you kidding?" Steph made a face. "I accidentally dropped my hairbrush into the toilet."

"Just be glad it wasn't your toothbrush," I teased her. "Hey, Brian, I have a fun fact for you."

"If it's more stuff about kidneys, I don't want to hear it," he said.

"Oh, come on," I said. "Can you believe that

kidneys have 140 miles of tubes and filters? I can't believe that there are 140 miles of anything in our bodies."

"Let's change the subject," Steph said.

Steph always gets kind of squeamish when Brian and I talk medical talk. "Okay, let's get going," I said.

We gathered up our saddles and equipment and went to the stalls to get our horses ready. Our coach, Gail Dutton, came over to us. "I'm really disappointed, Kelly. You haven't practiced much at all this month," she said.

"But my—" I stopped, deciding that I'd better not tell her about Allyson. She'd be mad if she knew I told more people. "I'm sorry," I mumbled. "I've been busy."

"I thought you were more dedicated, Kelly. And you know that you probably won't make the team unless your time is 14.2 or better," Gail said sternly.

"I know." I had been averaging that before Allyson got sick. "I'll try really hard."

The arena for western riding was set up for barrel racing. There were brightly-painted 55-gallon drums set up in a cloverleaf pattern. The grounds were already full of riders and horses and spectators.

When my turn came I suddenly felt nervous. I think my nervousness affected Sidekick, because he wasn't at a full gallop when I passed the timing light, like you're supposed to be. I knocked over the very first barrel, which gave me a five-second penalty. And when I tried to go around the second barrel, I swung too wide and lost more time. The whole ride was a complete disaster. I cringed when the announcer called out my time over the loudspeaker.

On my next two tries I did much better, but the first ride brought my score way down. The three of us waited anxiously for the announcement of who'd made the team. The loudspeaker squawked and I held my breath. Brian's name was called first for his age group. Steph made it, too. I waited patiently, but Kelly Reed was nowhere on the list.

"I'm really sorry, Kelly," Steph said.

"Me, too," Brian said. "You just had a bad day. It can happen to anybody."

"I couldn't concentrate on the race," I admitted, trying to pretend that it didn't matter if I missed out on the race. But it *did* matter. It hurt a lot.

"It won't be any fun without you," Steph said.

"Well," I said as brightly as I could, "it's not the end of the world. You two made the team." I fumbled in my pocket for a tissue and held up a handful of hay. "Sometimes I even find this stuff in my bed." Then my voice broke and I turned away. "I'd better get Sidekick back to his stall. I have to get home."

Brian handed me the red bandanna that he wore around his neck. I wiped my eyes.

"I'll go with you," he said. "I walk right by your house."

He always went right past my house, but this was the first time he'd offered to walk me home. I glanced at Steph. We usually left the center together.

"I have an errand to do," Steph said quickly. "Go ahead."

Brian helped me clean up Sidekick and brush his coat. I patted Sidekick's neck as we were leaving. "I'm sorry, pal," I said. "It wasn't your fault that we didn't make the team."

"Kelly, did you know that Babe Ruth, the famous baseball player, held the record for most home runs for a long time?" Brian asked.

I looked up at him. "No I didn't, but why should I care?"

"Because he also held the record for most strikeouts," he answered. "What I'm trying to say is that there will be other competitions. You had other things to worry about."

Brian always knew the right thing to say. "Thanks," I told him. "I'll remember that."

As Brian and I headed for home, he asked, "How's Allyson really doing?" he asked. "Nobody sees her anymore."

I glanced at him out of the corner of my eye. *Was Allyson the reason he'd asked to walk me home?*

"She's doing better," I said coolly.

He changed the subject. "I'm sorry about your not making the team. I know it's because you're worried about your sister."

"Yeah, I am," I said and sighed. "Some people die, even though they're on dialysis. I don't know what I'd do if—if—" I just couldn't talk about it.

Just then we walked by a pizza place and I saw Keith Harrison coming out with a huge pizza box. I took a deep breath and blocked his way.

"I want to talk to you," I said, not hiding my anger. I'd always liked Keith, but I wasn't happy at all that he'd been ignoring Ally—especially when she needed him.

"I don't have time right now, Kelly. Some friends are waiting for this pizza," he said.

"What about another friend of yours?" I asked, knowing that Allyson would be furious with me. But I'd gone too far to stop now.

"Maybe I'd better get going," Brian said, sounding embarrassed.

"No, I want you to stay," I said angrily. "Keith, did you hear about Allyson?"

He avoided my eyes. "I heard she was in the hospital," he mumbled.

"I suppose you heard she had cancer?" I asked.

"Yes. I'm sorry, Kelly. I really am, but—"

"You stupid creep!" I yelled. I'd never talked to a guy like that before, but I was mad—and getting madder! "If you would have called her, you'd know she doesn't have cancer at all."

Keith's head shot up. "You mean she's okay?"

"No, she's not okay. She had kidney failure, and she's on dialysis," I explained.

"Allyson told me about your grandmother and why you probably hadn't been around. Maybe she buys that excuse. Personally, I think it's a lousy reason for deserting a friend."

"Why didn't she call me?" Keith stammered. "If she cared about me, she'd have told me what was wrong."

"She's the one who's sick," I said. "Why should *she* have to call *you* for support?"

"My grandmother never wanted anyone around when she was sick. I guess I figured when Allyson didn't call, she was like Gran."

"Ally acts like that sometimes, but I know

she wants to see you," I said.

"I'm sorry Allyson's had a rough time." Keith looked at his watch. "I really have to go—"

"So, are you going to call her?" I pressed.

He sighed. "You're sure one stubborn girl. You're not a thing like your sister." I glared at him until he gave in. "Okay, okay, I'll call her tonight."

Brian was trying to stifle a laugh. He knew how stubborn I could be. "Good," I said, "but don't you dare tell her that I talked to you."

"I won't," Keith said. "Kelly," he added softly. "You're okay."

As Brian and I headed for home, he grinned at me. "Keith's right, you know. You're okay."

"It was nothing," I said. "I'd do anything for my sister."

*　*　*　*　*

The house was empty when I got home. I wished I'd asked Brian to come in and listen to music or watch TV. I wandered into Allyson's room to look at all her ribbons and trophies. There wouldn't be any for me this year. I ran my hand over Allyson's first medal.

"Hey, what are you doing in here?"

Feeling like I'd been caught stealing, I

turned around to see Allyson at the door. We had a rule in our house that no one goes into anyone's room without permission.

"Sorry, Ally. I—I was just looking at all your trophies and stuff," I said honestly.

"Well, you'll have one of your own pretty soon. How'd you do?"

"Rotten," I admitted. I turned away so she couldn't see my face. "I didn't make the team."

"What? How come?" she asked. "I've seen you ride. You're good."

"Not good enough." I shrugged. "It's no big deal."

I had to get out of there before I cried. After all, how could I be so upset about missing out on one stupid competition? Look at everything that Ally was going through.

"I'll see you later," I said. "I have to go call Steph."

Steph came over after dinner so we could study together. We sat on the floor, leaning against the foot of my brass bed. Neither one of us mentioned barrel racing or the competition. We got out our math books but we talked about a new guy in our class. Allyson's bedroom was right across from mine. I kept listening for her phone to ring.

"Are you waiting for somebody?" Steph asked. "You keep looking at the door."

"I think Keith is going to call Ally tonight," I whispered. Steph knew about the way he'd treated my sister. "I talked to him today and chewed him out for dropping her."

"She'll probably hang up on him. I would," Steph said.

I frowned. I hadn't thought of that. "Do you think I should have told Allyson what I did?"

"I don't know. Does she still like him?"

"I think so," I said.

The way Keith and Allyson met was so romantic. She'd been out riding when a snake spooked her horse and threw her. She wasn't really hurt, but this gorgeous guy came along and took her home. I think she pretended to be hurt worse just so he'd stay around. He did and they've been going together ever since.

When the phone finally did ring, I jumped up and went out into the hall. Steph followed right behind me. "Shh," I hissed. Allyson's bedroom door was open a little. Her voice sounded cold and unfriendly, but at least she hadn't hung up on him.

Steph and I sneaked closer to Allyson's door.

"After all this time," Allyson was saying, "why did you call tonight?"

"Because of me," I whispered to Steph.

"Just a minute, Keith," Ally said.

There was total silence, then I saw Allyson standing at the door glaring at us. "This is a private conversation," she said to us. Then the door slammed shut.

In a fit of giggles, Steph and I ran back to my room. "I think I did it," I said. "I'll bet they're going to get back together."

"What a matchmaker," she said. "But we'd better do some real studying or we're both going to flunk that math test on Monday."

We studied for an hour, then Steph had to leave. I couldn't wait to find out what happened between Ally and Keith. I knocked on Ally's closed door.

"It's me," I said.

"Come in, Miss Nosey," she said. Allyson was lying on her bed with her hands behind her head. She was smiling.

"Who was that?" I asked, trying to act innocent.

"It was Keith. He apologized for not calling. I apologized for not telling him I was sick. We're even now."

I sat at the foot of her bed. "Then everything's okay between you?"

"Why're you so interested?" She gave me a suspicious look. "Hey, did you have anything to do with his calling me?"

"Uh—" I stammered. "What did Keith say?"

She thought for a minute. "Actually, he never said why he hadn't called." She looked at me again. "It was you. You talked to him, didn't you?"

"Uh—just for a minute. I happened to bump into him in front of the pizza place and your name just happened to come up. Don't be mad. I was just trying to help."

"It's okay, Kell. I'll bet you really told him off, didn't you?"

I hung my head, but I couldn't help grinning. "I called him a jerk and a stupid creep. I guess I was pretty rough on him."

We both burst out laughing. It felt great to be acting like sisters again.

"Kelly," she said more seriously. "I know you didn't make the barrel racing team because you've been worried about me." She hopped off the bed and walked over to the wall of trophies and took down her first-place trophy. She held it out to me. "I want you to have this. You deserve it."

"But that's your favorite—"

She touched my lips to silence me. "Nobody deserves a medal more than you do, Kelly."

My throat closed tight. I couldn't say a word. She had given me one of her favorite things. What could I ever give her in return?

Six

ALLYSON hated the dialysis machine. Even worse, she hated having Mom poke the huge needles into her arm. Sometimes she got really dizzy and sick while she was using the machine. Mom had to take her blood pressure every half hour.

Once I got used to seeing her blood going in and out of the tubes, I thought it was kind of interesting. Mom had to stay in the room the whole time to be sure that nothing went wrong. Allyson's blood pressure could rise so high or fall so low that she could pass out. Or there was the chance that air could get into the line and into her blood. And we had to make sure that her veins didn't collapse.

I liked to sit with Allyson while she was on the machine. I figured it might keep her from getting too bored and irritated with the whole thing. It was the least I could do. In fact, it was the only thing I was allowed to do for my sister. Most of the time I didn't even feel like part of the family. Sometimes I wondered if *I* got sick, would anyone besides Ally even notice?

One Sunday before dinner, Allyson and I were listening to music and looking at teen magazines. Ally was on dialysis. She chewed on ice so she wouldn't drink too much fluid. Dad was working late and Mom was going over some papers. Allyson was stretched out in her new yellow recliner. Yellow is her favorite color. She says it makes her feel good. I felt depressed and I guess I wasn't hiding it very well.

"What's wrong?" Allyson asked. "You're awfully quiet."

I didn't want to tell her that this was the weekend of the competition in Sacramento.

"Nothing's wrong," I lied.

"Are you sure?"

"Sure, I'm sure."

"It wouldn't be because Brian hasn't been around here much lately, would it?" she asked softly.

"Of course not. It's not me he comes to see anyhow."

"Oh?" She raised an eyebrow.

"I suppose you don't know he has a crush on you?" I asked.

She gave me that look again.

63

"It's true, Ally. Who does he talk to when he's here? He thinks of me like a sister." I made a face.

"Yeah, right," she said sarcastically.

"Ally, stop teasing," I said.

Mom broke in. "Kelly, would you get something for me? The Stevenson contract is in the left-hand drawer of my desk."

"Sure." Ever since Allyson started home dialysis, I've been the family gofer. This was the third time Mom had sent me to get something that day. I was considering roller skates.

I looked in the left-hand drawer but there wasn't any contract for the Stevensons. I checked the top drawer and then the right-hand drawer. Finally, I gave up and trudged back to the bedroom.

"I'm sorry, Mom, but I can't find it," I said.

"I'm sure it's there. Will you look one more time? Your dad needs it. He's going to stop by for it," Mom said.

I headed back to the study. I checked every drawer in the desk. I even looked under the desk. There was nothing.

"I still can't find it," I told Mom.

"Oh, Kelly," she complained. "You know I don't like to leave Allyson while she's on dialysis."

"I'll be fine," Allyson said. "I know what to do and Kelly's here with me."

"Sure," I said. "I've been watching how everything works."

Mom hesitated. "I guess nothing can happen in a couple of minutes."

I settled myself on the floor where I could watch all the flashing lights on the machine.

"Mom's such a worrywart," Allyson said. She leaned over and stretched to reach a magazine that had dropped on the floor.

"Hey, let me get that," I said.

"Never mind. I've got it," she said. "Did you see that article on modeling? It sounds like fun."

"Yeah, but I'd never want to do that," I said.

"You're lucky, Kelly," Allyson said.

"Why?" I had no idea what she was talking about.

"I wish I was like you. You've known since you were six that you wanted to be a doctor. I don't have any idea what I want to be—especially now." She nodded toward the machine.

"You could—" I began, but Ally's shriek stopped me.

"Kelly!"

Her yell brought me off the floor. "What's wrong?"

"My arm! The needle's slipped!"

I rushed over to her. The place on her arm where the tubes were attached had started to swell. I could see blood going into the tissue.

"Mom!" I screamed. "Help!"

"Turn the knob," Allyson yelled, her voice panicky.

I looked at the machine, frantically trying to figure out what I was supposed to do. "Which knob?" I asked. If I didn't turn the right one, something else might go wrong! "Allyson, which knob?"

"Kelly, I..." I glanced over at her. Her face had turned white and her head fell forward. She looked limp, as if she had fainted.

I ran to the door and screamed, "Mom! Come quick!"

Mom came running down the hall. "What's wrong?"

"The needle slipped. Ally's passed out!" I cried. "Look at her arm."

By now, Allyson's arm had a knot on it the size of a golf ball. Mom quickly turned the right knob. "Didn't you hear the alarm on the machine?" she asked as she lowered Allyson's chair.

I shook my head. "I didn't hear anything." My heart was beating in my ears.

The pump on the machine stopped working, turning the blood flow off. Mom brought Allyson around and gave her extra fluid.

"I knew I shouldn't have left the room,"

Mom said. "Kelly, fill the ice bag and bring it to me."

As I rushed to the kitchen and got ice cubes, I felt sick inside. The first time I got to do something important, I blew it. Mom trusted me and I'd let her down. Some doctor I'd make!

When I came back with the ice bag, Mom had already reinserted the needle in a new place in the graft. She'd given Allyson some medicine for low blood pressure.

I went over to her and knelt on the floor beside her chair. "Are you okay, Ally?"

She nodded weakly.

"I was so scared," I said. "I'm sorry I couldn't help you."

"I was scared, too, but it wasn't your fault, Kell. I shouldn't have moved my arm the way I did."

Mom shook her head. "No, it's my fault. I didn't have the machine set right. That's why the alarm didn't go off. Kelly, I'm going to teach you how to use the machine. Then we can check each other so we don't make any more mistakes." She turned to Allyson. "Honey, I'm so sorry."

"It's not any of our fault," Allyson said angrily. "I just hate everything about this stupid kidney disease!"

"Allyson!" Mom said sternly. "Talking like

that isn't going to help anything. You have to be positive."

"I don't care." Allyson's face was flushed. "I hate it. I'm going to talk to Dr. Metzger about having a transplant."

Mom and I looked at each other in surprise. I knew that neither Mom nor Dad was crazy about the idea. I think they were scared about trying anything that could be risky.

"I thought you were afraid of having the operation," I said.

"I hate having these needles poked into me. I'm tired of feeling crummy all the time. If I had the operation, I'd only be in the hospital for a week or so. Then I'd have a normal life again."

"It's your decision, honey," Mom told her. "Give this plenty of thought."

I didn't have to think about it. It was a great idea. My sister wanted a normal life. And so did I.

I called Steph as soon as I could to tell her about the transplant. She answered the phone.

"It's me. Kelly," I said.

"I know your voice," she said coldly.

"Is this a bad time to talk?" I asked. "I know it's kind of late."

"Oh, it's late, all right."

She definitely sounded sarcastic. What was

going on? "Did I do something to make you mad, Steph?" I asked.

"You didn't do anything," she replied, sounding just as cold.

Had I forgotten something? Then, suddenly, the answer flashed into my mind. *The competition!*

"When did you get back from Sacramento?" I asked.

"Yesterday," she said.

I remembered I'd promised that I'd call her as soon as she got back to get the details.

"Steph, I'm sorry. We had an emergency with Allyson. I forgot everything else. How'd you do? What was your time?"

The line was silent and then she said, "I didn't think you were interested."

"Interested? Steph, I really want to know."

"Brian and I both won medals," she said. "I beat my best time ever by two seconds. Brian did great, too. The whole team did."

"I'm glad for you," I said honestly.

"I wish you'd been there," she said softly.

"Me, too, but I'm glad things went well. I guess I'd better call Brian, too, before it gets too late. I'll see you in the morning."

After I hung up, I realized I hadn't told Steph about the transplant. Maybe it was just as well that I didn't tell anyone, not even Steph. Allyson probably wouldn't want me to tell anyone—not just yet anyway.

*   *   *   *   *

Once Allyson decided to have the transplant, she seemed to handle the dialysis better. Over the next few weeks, she invited her friends over and started riding again. She began doing some of the things she used to do. I was glad that she was seeing her friends again, but I kind of missed our times alone together.

Dr. Metzger began to test Ally to determine if she'd be a good candidate for a transplant. She met the transplant team: the surgeon, the transplant coordinator, who was like the quarterback of the team, a psychologist, a social worker, a dietician, a physical therapist, and even a religious counselor. They explained to her and Mom and Dad all the pluses of a transplant. They also told her about all the things that could go wrong.

The team was looking to see if Allyson had a good attitude. They said that was really important. They wanted to be sure that if her body did reject the new kidney, that she could go back on dialysis until another kidney was found.

Allyson had to have all kinds of tests. They did tests on her heart, lungs, bones, stomach, and just about every part of her body. Mom and Dad were both tested to see if their blood and tissue types matched Allyson's. She has a rare blood type, but we were hoping that one of them would be a good match. We knew that it took a while for the results to come through.

When Christmastime rolled around, I was happy that our family was big on birthdays and holidays. It was a chance for all of us to be together. Grandma Allyson and her sister, my great aunt, came to visit at Christmas, just like they always do.

"I weigh everything Allyson eats," Mom was saying on Christmas Eve as she peeled potatoes. All of us were in the kitchen helping to get stuff ready for Christmas dinner. "She can only have four cups of fluid a day—and that includes things like gravy and ice cream."

"Poor girl," Grandma said. "It must be so hard for her."

"I cook all her food separately," Mom said. "I don't use any salt. That's why I'm going to soak these potatoes overnight to leach out the sodium and potassium."

"Mom," Ally said. "I've told you a million times you don't have to go to all that trouble. I'll just eat a tiny bit of everything."

I felt sorry for Allyson. She wouldn't get to pig out on all the goodies. She sure got a lot of attention, though.

"Sweetheart," Grandma Allyson said to Ally, "You look tired."

"I'm fine, Grandma."

Allyson gave my leg a little kick and I tried not to smile. Ever since Grandma and Aunt Fran arrived the night before, they'd treated Ally like a baby. They hovered over her until she must have felt smothered.

Ally acted as if she didn't like all the attention, but I kind of envied her. Grandma Allyson came over to the table and looked at Ally.

"You're pale and you've lost weight," she said. Tears welled up in her eyes. "I just feel so awful about your illness. Are you able to ride anymore?"

"Not as much," Ally said.

Nobody even mentioned that I hadn't made the barrel race team.

"It isn't fair that a beautiful young girl should have to suffer," Grandma said.

Ally fingered the new silver chain that Grandma had given her this morning.

"I'll be okay once I get the transplant," Ally said.

"Are you sure this kidney transplant thing is right for Allyson?" Aunt Fran asked Mom. "I'm not sure I approve of all this experimenting."

72

"It's not experimenting, Aunt Fran," Ally said. "They've been doing kidney transplants for over 35 years. With a kidney from either Mom or Dad, I have a good chance of not rejecting it."

Aunt Fran was silent for a minute, then she said, "I still think it goes against nature," as if that settled the matter.

Grandma glared at her. "You mean you wouldn't give me a kidney if I needed one?"

"You don't need one, so I'm not going to *what if* with you."

Grandma and Aunt Fran always had friendly arguments.

"If it came right down to it, I think you'd give me your kidney," Grandma said.

"Just think of all the lives that have been saved. The success rate of transplants is up to between 70 and 90 percent," I put in. But nobody paid any attention to me.

"It's Allyson's decision," Mom said. "If she wants the transplant, we're behind her 100 per—"

The telephone cut her off. Dad answered it.

"Did either of us match?" I heard Dad ask. His shoulders slumped. "Oh. We were hoping...yes...we appreciate your telling us so we didn't have to wait until after the holiday. Yes, I'll tell her. Good-bye."

He slowly hung up the receiver and sighed. He went to Allyson and put his arm around her. "Honey, I'm sorry. Neither your mother nor I are a good tissue match. The doctor said he'd put your name on the waiting list."

"It could be years before they find a good match," Allyson cried angrily and ran from the room. I hurt for her and there was nothing I could do or say to make it easier.

Grandma started to follow her. "She'd rather be alone now, Mother," Dad said. "I'm afraid she was putting too much hope on our being compatible. A family member has the best chance for a match, especially since she has an unusual blood type."

"I'm going to get tested," Grandma Allyson said.

"They wouldn't take you," Dad said. "Not with the heart trouble you've had."

What about me? I wanted to scream. For once in my life I could do something really important. What a Christmas gift that would be! Suddenly, I was so excited about my idea that I could hardly talk.

"Mom? Dad?" I blurted out. "I want to give one of my kidneys to Allyson," I announced.

They all slowly turned their heads to look at me. I couldn't tell if they were excited, shocked, horrified, or what. But inside, I felt like I'd just come up with the idea of the year.

Seven

"**A**BSOLUTELY not," Mom said.

"But Mom! A sister or brother has the best chance of making a good match," I said. "The only thing better would be a twin and I can't help with that."

Dad shook his head. "You're too young, Kelly."

"I know you're supposed to be eighteen, but let me talk to the doctor," I pleaded. "I'll bet I can talk him into letting me do it."

"You can't make such an important decision," Grandma Allyson said. "You're too young."

Allyson was her namesake and also her favorite grandchild. If anybody, I thought sure she'd be all for it.

"Mom, you told me I was grown up for my age," I argued. "Besides, it's my body. Don't I have any say what I do with it?"

"This is entirely different," she said. "This

could affect your whole life."

"I don't see why I can't do it if I want," I said. "You all treat me like I'm a baby."

"I think it's wonderful that you want to help your sister," Mom said. "But it is risky and I don't think Allyson would let you do it."

"The doctors probably wouldn't either," Dad said.

"Maybe they will. Please let me try," I pleaded. "If I can convince them, will you let me get tested?"

"I don't know," Mom said. "We'll have to do a lot of thinking before we answer that."

"Okay. But I'm going to go ask Ally right now."

I hurried to Allyson's room. She was lying on the bed. "Ally, I have a great idea, but you have to agree."

"I don't feel like talking now, Kell." She sounded so discouraged.

"I know how bad you must feel. That's why I want you to hear my idea." I blurted out my idea and added, "It's a Christmas present."

I waited for her to say, *Kelly, that's so wonderful of you. You're the best sister anybody ever had.*

"Forget it, Kelly," Ally said flatly. "I could never let you do it."

"Why not? You probably wouldn't reject my kidney because we're sisters. Otherwise, it could take years on the waiting list."

She sat up and looked at me intently. "I read in one of my books that kids have to get a court order to donate," she said slowly.

"Why didn't you tell me that before?" I asked.

"Because I would never have asked you to do that for me, Kell," she said. "I don't want you to feel like you have to do this for me."

"I *know* I don't have to do it," I said. "*I want to*. But we still have to convince Mom, Dad, and the doctors."

She got up and went over to the window. A few drops of rain spattered against the panes. "I hate the rain," she whispered. "Why can't it ever snow for Christmas here?" Then she turned to me. "No, Kelly. I can't let you give up a kidney for me. What if you got kidney disease someday and you needed that kidney?"

"Then I'd go on dialysis until I could get a transplant," I said simply. "At least let me try, Ally."

She came over to me and gave me a hug. I finally heard the words I'd been waiting for. "Kelly Annabel Reed, you're the best sister in the whole world."

* * * * *

That night I lay awake for a long time. Maybe it was the excitement of Christmas and of opening presents. I didn't think so, though. For some reason, I was scared—really scared.

Grandpa Hendrix had died during surgery. I guess it scared me knowing that I could die from surgery—and I wasn't even sick. I knew from all the pamphlets and articles I'd read that donors hardly ever had serious problems. But I felt stuck. Maybe I shouldn't have been so eager to tell Allyson my idea.

Finally, I fell asleep. But I had a terrible nightmare about an alien creature who was trying to tear out my heart. I woke up as it started to get light outside.

I needed to talk to Stephie. She had her own phone, so I hoped that she'd answer before the rest of her family woke up. It rang three times before I heard her say, "Hello?"

"Steph, it's me."

"What's wrong? It's so early," she groaned.

"I don't want to talk on the phone," I said. "The center's not open today, so we can't ride. Let's go for a walk."

"Kelly, I just looked out the window. It's barely light outside and it's raining."

"It's important," I said quietly.

"Okay, what's a little rain? I'll meet you at the lake by the duck bench in 10 minutes."

I left a note on the kitchen table saying

where I was going. I grabbed my jacket, some old bread, and headed for Lake Corina. The wind was blowing leaves into the streets.

Steph and I lived on opposite sides of the man-made lake, so we always met at the metal bench on one end. A family of ducks usually congregated near it.

I got there first and began tossing bits of bread in the water, trying to sort out my muddled thoughts.

"Why are you wasting bread?" Stephie asked, startling me. "There isn't a duck in sight." She grinned. "They're still asleep—like any normal person would be on Christmas morning. Except for little kids, that is."

"Merry Christmas, Steph. Thanks for the CD. I love it."

"Me, too." We both laughed because we'd given each other the exact same gift.

"What else did you get?" she asked.

"Steph, I really need to talk."

She sat down beside me on the wet bench. "Is it your sister? Is she worse?"

"No, she's okay, but it is about her."

"So, spit it out, Kell. What's wrong?"

"I think I opened my mouth too soon. I offered to give Allyson one of my kidneys. And now I'm scared," I said.

Her mouth was open. "No kidding? You really offered her a kidney?"

"Yeah, I told everybody—Mom, Dad, Grandma, and Aunt Fran. And worst of all, I told Allyson."

"Didn't you mean it?" Stephie asked.

"Sure I meant it. Then I started thinking about it. I'm not sure I can do it," I said.

"Just say you changed your mind," Steph suggested.

"I can't do that. We just found out that Mom and Dad aren't a good match for her. You should have seen Ally's face when I told her my idea."

"How come you said it in the first place?" Steph asked.

"Because I wanted to do something important. And because I really want to help Ally," I explained.

"It's sure scary, though," Steph agreed.

I nodded. "Maybe it wouldn't be so bad, after all. I'm healthy and I know we have the same blood type."

"I really admire you, Kell. That's just about the greatest thing I've ever heard. I bet you'd be in the newspaper and everything."

"Maybe Allyson and I would be on TV. I wonder what it feels like to be a celebrity," I said.

"I'd tell everybody you're my very best friend," Stephie said, sounding excited about the whole idea. "And I'd come to see you every day in the hospital."

Hospital? Surgery? "I don't know, Steph. What if I have a terrible scar? What if I can't ever wear a bikini again?"

"Some one-piece suits are cool," Steph said.

"Sure." I felt crummy for having doubts. I was really selfish to be worrying about a bikini when my sister was scared about her whole life. "What's more important? A scar or Allyson?"

"Right," she said.

"What's right?" a voice behind me asked.

I turned around to see Brian. "Hi," I said. "What're you doing out here in the rain?"

"Merry Christmas to you, too," he said with a grin.

"I'm sorry," I said. "I was just surprised to see you."

"I went to your house first. Your dad said you'd left a note saying you were here. So, what's right?" he asked again.

"Kelly's going to give one of her kidneys to her sister," Steph said before I could answer. "Isn't that the greatest?"

"I think it stinks," Brian said bluntly.

I stared at him in surprise. He liked Ally. Why wouldn't he want her to have a transplant? It could save her life.

"Why does it stink?" I demanded.

"It just does," he said.

81

"You sound like my aunt," I said, getting a little mad. "Luckily, it's not up to you," I said coldly. "I'm going to do it."

He pulled a package from beneath his rain jacket and shoved it at me. "Merry Christmas," he said and took off at a jog.

We both watched him until he was out of sight. I looked at the heavy package wrapped in plastic. "We've never given each other presents before."

"Knowing him, it could be a gag gift," Stephie said.

"You're probably right." I was still mad. "I can't believe he said that."

"Maybe he's worried about you," she said softly.

No way. He liked Ally. "No, it can't be that."

The rain started to come down harder. "We'd better go," I said. "Thanks for listening, Steph."

"Are you going to go through with it?"

I hesitated a second. "Yes, I really am," I said firmly.

"Let me know as soon as you find out when it's going to be. I'll be your press agent and call the newspapers and TV people. Who knows?" she said with a grin. "You could be famous."

"Famous? I like the sound of that," I said and grinned.

Eight

AS soon as I got home, I opened Brian's present. But it wasn't a gag gift at all. It was a book on trivia. I couldn't figure out why he'd give me a present and not Ally. Could Steph be right? Was it possible that Brian liked me?

I helped Aunt Fran prepare our usual Christmas breakfast. She always brought her Belgian waffle iron and my favorite homemade raspberry syrup. I knew she was really against my giving Ally a kidney. I figured I could score points by showing her how responsible I was.

While we were all eating, I brought up the subject of the transplant again. "You're going to let me give Allyson one of my kidneys, aren't you?" I asked Mom and Dad. "Ally said it's okay with her."

"Is that true?" Mom asked, looking at Ally.

"I didn't exactly say *yes*, but if Kelly is sure about it, then it's okay with me if she's tested," Ally said. "I want her to be really sure though, because my body might end up rejecting her kidney. Besides, the court has to agree to it before it goes very far."

"Well, thank goodness there's somebody to protect children," Aunt Fran said. "Allyson, how will you feel if you reject Kelly's kidney? You can't give it back to her when you're done with it."

Ally thought for a long time. "I guess I'd feel terrible for myself, but even worse for her."

"You wouldn't need to feel that way," I said. "When you give a gift, you don't ask for it back, do you?"

Mom and Dad looked at each other. Mom smiled a little. They each nodded.

"Yahoo," I cried.

"Don't get so excited," Dad said. "We have to talk to the transplant team. Don't get your hopes up yet," he said, looking back and forth between Ally and me. "And we have to get past the court—somehow."

"I'll do whatever it takes," I said. "I just hope we can do it soon."

* * * * *

Soon turned into weeks of waiting. I'd wanted to get it all over with before the weather got nicer. I knew that I needed lots of practice for the next time I could try out for the barrel race team.

But it wasn't easy to find time to practice. It took a lot of time to convince the doctors that donating a kidney was my idea. I guess some parents make kids feel like they have to do it. I wasn't even allowed to have the tests to see if I'd be a good match for Ally until we got the court order.

It was mid-March before we met with the judge. A late storm blew in from the ocean. We didn't have too much bad weather in southern California, but today the streets were flooded from the strong winds and rain.

Ally and I were excused from school. Dr. Metzger and a social worker met us at the courthouse. As we walked into the courtroom, I felt like a criminal on trial. Even though the room was cold, I started to sweat, especially when we were sworn in. I was scared, but I tried not to show it.

Judge Parker looked seven feet tall in her long black robe. She wore her glasses down over her nose. She stared at us over the top of the silver rims. She looked so serious.

It seemed to take forever for her to read all the declarations we'd had to sign. Allyson wanted a kidney. I wanted to give mine. Why did it have to take so long to decide? Then the judge asked me to come into her chambers. In a panic, I looked back and forth between Mom, Dad, and Allyson.

"It'll be all right," Dad said. "Just tell the judge how you feel."

As I walked into the judge's chambers, she nodded for me to take a seat. She took off her robe and sat behind a desk. In her floral dress, she looked more human somehow. I relaxed a little.

She asked me a million questions. I tried to answer honestly. After all, I'd sworn to tell the truth. Finally, Judge Parker cleared her throat. "I want you to know that this is not an easy decision, Kelly," she said. "The doctor assures me that if Allyson receives a kidney from a sibling, the chances for a successful transplant are greatly increased."

I nodded.

"I'm convinced that this is your decision and that your parents aren't pushing you into this," she said. "I don't feel that they are putting one daughter's welfare above the other. And I also don't think they'll blame you if the transplant fails. Kelly, you're young, but you seem to understand what's involved."

"I'm going to be a doctor," I said, breaking in. Then I realized that I'd interrupted her. "I'm sorry, Your Honor. I didn't mean to interrupt."

"I think it's wonderful that you want to be a doctor," she said. "And it's easy to see that you like to help people."

"You are going to say yes, aren't you? Oh, please," I pleaded.

She stood up and put on her robe. "Let's go back into the courtroom now and I'll give my decision there."

My heart sank. She was going to say no. I just knew it. If she was going to say yes, she would have told me right then and there. I felt terrible for Ally. Now she'd have to go on the waiting list. I hurried back to Allyson.

"How did it go?" she whispered.

"I don't know. Ally, please don't be too disappointed if the judge says no."

Allyson reached out, took my hand, and squeezed it. "I don't want *you* to feel bad if she says no," Ally whispered. "I'll never forget that you wanted to try."

The judge took her seat, but didn't say anything. Because I thought she was going to say no, I had a strange, momentary feeling of relief. The feeling startled me, and I pushed it aside. Of course I wanted her to say yes.

"After careful consideration, I've made my decision," the judge said.

I closed my eyes.

"Petition granted," the judge said.

I opened my eyes, let out a little whoop of

87

joy, and hugged Allyson as hard as I could. "There's more," the judge said. "If Kelly's blood and tissue types are compatible with Allyson's, I want both girls to be thoroughly evaluated psychologically."

Dr. Metzger assured her that we'd both go through intensive testing to make sure we were fit physically and mentally. Ally started to cry as we were leaving the courtroom. Dad put his arms around both of us. "How about celebrating, girls? Ally, you go on dialysis tonight, so I think you could splurge a little."

I couldn't resist spouting a bit of trivia. "Did you know that the average person scarfs down a ton of food and drink a year?"

Dad laughed. "Just don't try to do it in one day."

"Can you believe it?" Allyson asked. "Soon I won't have to use that machine anymore!"

That afternoon, we were like a real family again. We laughed over everything. Dad cracked old jokes we'd heard a million times, but they seemed hysterically funny now. Mom didn't look tired. Allyson was almost giddy— you know, all giggly and silly. It was the best day we'd had since Allyson got sick.

* * * * *

I had the blood and tissue test. And like

I'd hoped, Ally and I were compatible. After that, I had more blood tests, X-rays, and tons of other tests to determine if my heart and blood vessels were strong enough. The doctor wanted to make sure both my kidneys were healthy. He said that after the operation my one kidney would get bigger and take over the work of two.

My trivia book said the average waiting time in a doctor's office is 20 minutes. Ha! It seemed like I'd been waiting about 20 years! Then I felt guilty for being impatient, with everything that Ally had been through. A little waiting wasn't going to hurt me.

Each of us had to talk to a social worker. I walked over to his office one day after school. The social worker didn't look scary at all. He leaned back in his chair with his hands behind his head. His name was Matt, and I liked him right away. I was kind of nervous at first, but it was easy talking to him.

I almost blew it when he asked me why I wanted to give Allyson one of my kidneys. I almost told him it was because I wanted to do something really important, so everybody would be as proud of me as they were of Ally. But that would have been the wrong thing to say. Luckily, I didn't say it.

"I'd do anything for my sister," I said. "She's done everything for me. She's taught me to dance and wear makeup and talk to guys, and she helps me with my riding. She takes my side when I get into an argument with Mom or Dad. I mean, she's terrific."

"It sounds like you're good friends," he said. "Don't you ever fight?"

"Oh, sure," I said, then stopped. Maybe that was the wrong answer. "Once in a while. She gets mad if I borrow her clothes without asking her."

He nodded. "My brother used to get upset when I took his baseball glove without asking."

"Just because we get mad at each other once in a while—that won't keep us from going through with the transplant, will it?" I asked.

He gave me a reassuring smile. "No, it just means you're two normal teenagers. I'd worry more if you told me everything was perfect between you. Do you ever get upset with her?"

I thought for a minute. "She used to hog the phone before she got her own. Sometimes she gets mad and won't tell me what's wrong. But she's easy to get along with, though. Everybody likes her."

"Are you a little jealous of her sometimes?" he asked.

Uh-oh. I thought for a second. "I don't think so. But I do wish I could do all the things she's good at," I admitted.

"Kelly, you're fourteen now. Do you think you'll feel the same way about the transplant when you're grown up? What if you have a daughter who needs a kidney and you can't give one. Will you resent Allyson?"

"I'd feel pretty bad," I answered. "But by then I'm sure medicine will be more advanced. And maybe there will be more donors by then."

"Do you know what rejection means in a transplant?" he asked.

"I guess so. The body thinks there's something that doesn't belong there and says 'Get out!'"

"Something like that. Antibodies try to destroy the foreign tissue. We have powerful drugs now that prevent the immune system from rejecting the kidney."

I nodded. We had studied about the immune system in biology class.

"How will you feel if Allyson rejects your kidney?" Matt asked. "There is that possibility, you know. Will you blame her?"

"Everybody asks me that," I said. "I read in one of Ally's books that some donors act as if the kidney was still theirs. They say stuff like, 'That's my kidney and you'd better not do anything to hurt it.' I think that's dumb. I gave Allyson a sweater this Christmas. But I didn't tell her where to wear it."

He grinned. "Dr. Metzger warned me that you knew a lot about transplants. He was right."

"Well, sure. I like to know about stuff. My friend Brian and I are always trying to get each other on trivia questions."

"How does Brian feel about your donating a kidney?" Matt asked.

I didn't answer for a minute. "Some people are for it. Some against," I said. "It's my decision."

"You're right," he said. "Kelly, I have one last question. This may sound strange, but please tell me your honest feelings. Would you go into a burning building to save your sister?"

"Sure," I said quickly.

"You realize that you can change your mind—even if it's a few days before surgery. I don't think Allyson would want you to go through with this if you have any doubts," Matt said.

My stomach started to churn, partly from excitement and partly from fear. I could tell he was really going to let me go ahead with it. I was scared, but I kept telling myself that I wanted to help Ally more than anything else in the world.

"Don't worry," I said firmly. "I won't change my mind."

Nine

THE transplant was a go! Steph and I had been working out almost every day at the equestrian center. Dad had been helping us get ready for the next competition. Even though I didn't make the team, I could still enter as an individual entry. I was hoping if I entered on my own and did well, the coach might let me on the team.

I was getting my fastest times ever. If I kept on, I might even beat Brian. But I would be cutting it awfully close. Surgery was at the beginning of May and the first big competition was at the end of May. I wanted to get the surgery over with so I'd be able to ride Sidekick in the competition.

"Why do we have to wait so long?" I asked Dr. Metzger one day.

"We still have to give Allyson several transfusions of your blood," he explained.

Using my best Count Dracula accent, I said, "My sister, the vampire."

He was used to me. He just smiled and said, "The transfusions will lessen the chances of rejection. Also, you and Allyson are out of school that month. The timing is perfect."

Not for me, it wasn't. Allyson and I are both in year-round schools, something we have out here in California. We go three months, then have a whole month off, instead of a regular summer vacation. I had big plans for May, and they sure didn't include being in the hospital.

Things were pretty normal around our house. Allyson acted more like herself. She didn't even seem to mind the dialysis so much. She had to wear more makeup than before, because she was so pale. The only real problem, though, seemed to be her blood pressure. Even with medicine it kept climbing. Sometimes she complained about her heart beating unevenly, but I just figured that happened because Keith was around. Believe me, he was around a lot.

But as May got closer, I began to get a sick feeling in my stomach every time I thought about the transplant. I never told anybody, though. Then, a couple of weeks before the operations, Steph and I were sitting cross-legged on her bed. We were listening to a new CD. The song wasn't really sad, and I don't know what happened, but all of a sudden I burst into tears.

"Kelly, what's wrong? Are you sick?" she asked.

I could only shake my head.

"Is there something I can do?" Steph grabbed a handful of tissues and gave them to me. "What is it, Kell? You can tell me."

Angrily, I brushed the tears away. "I don't know, I don't know," I cried. "My stomach's all in a knot and my chest feels like Sidekick is sitting on it."

"Are you worried about the operation?" she asked. "I sure wouldn't blame you if you were. It's scary."

"I didn't think I was," I said through my tears. "I just want to have it all over with. Maybe it's the waiting. I never thought it would take this long. I guess I've got too much time to sit around and think about it."

All the things people had said against my donating a kidney flooded back. *What if the one kidney you have left stops working? What if a child of yours needs a kidney someday? What if...? What if...?*

"Steph, I'm scared. My grandfather died in the hospital. I might die, too."

"You told me that the donors hardly ever have any problems."

"I know," I said, breaking into tears again. "But what if I'm one of those few?"

Stephie had started to cry too. "When you first told me, I thought it was a neat idea. I've made all these plans to get interviews with the newspaper and radio." She looked at me, sniffling like a baby. "But maybe you shouldn't go through with it after all."

My heart leaped up to my throat at her suggestion, then fell to my stomach. "Oh, I can't back out now," I moaned miserably. "Not after all the tests and the court order. I just can't do that to Ally."

"She's doing okay on dialysis, isn't she?"

"Yeah, I guess. Except for high blood pressure. Steph, she's really looking forward to the transplant. It's all she talks about, all the things she's going to do when the transplant is over."

"So she'll have to go on the waiting list. If you hadn't been a good match, that's what she would have done."

I didn't say anything for a minute. "Maybe I'm afraid I won't be well enough to compete at the end of May. Maybe I'm just being selfish. Oh, Steph, I don't know what to do!" I said and started sobbing again.

"You're not selfish at all," Steph said. "If you have too many doubts, I don't think you should do it."

"Matt—he's the social worker—*did* say I could back out."

"There you go," she said. "That means other people must change their minds, too."

"You're right, but other people aren't me. I always try to keep my word."

Feeling as if my insides were being torn apart, I wandered over to the window. I leaned my flushed face against the cool pane. Matt *had* said I could change my mind.

"What're you going to do?" Steph asked.

"I don't know. I'm not sure I could tell Allyson. Maybe I'll call Aunt Fran and talk to her. She's against it. Anyway, I have to get home."

"Call me and let me know what you decide. Okay?"

I sighed. "If I don't do it, it blows the one important thing I ever had a chance to do."

As I was leaving, I gave Steph a hug. "I'm sorry I dumped all my problems on you. Thanks, Steph."

I took the long way home, trying to make up my mind. I kept going over all the reasons why I should and shouldn't go through with it. Maybe I could get a bad cold or the measles or something—that would put off the surgery for a while. I kicked a pebble into the lake. No good. That would only postpone the surgery, not cancel it. No, I had to tell Allyson how I felt.

The setting sun reflected on the water. The sweet smell of honeysuckle filled the air. A mama duck with her eight babies swam toward me, looking for food.

"I'm sorry, guys, I don't have anything for you." Tears sprang to my eyes again. "I'm letting everybody down today," I whispered. I forced myself to head for home. It was my night to help with dinner. I'd decided I'd try to tell Allyson right after we ate.

The front door was unlocked. I went right to the kitchen. The makings for lasagna were on the counter. *Mom must be in the study,* I thought. I set the table and made a tossed salad. We usually had garlic bread with lasagna, so I went to the study to ask if she wanted me to get it ready.

"Mom?" Getting no answer, I pushed open the door. "Mom, should I—" The room was empty. Weird.

I checked Allyson's room, the bathrooms, the backyard. Nobody was home. It sure wasn't like Mom to go off and leave meat sitting out. I figured she probably had to rush down to the office for something.

I went back to the kitchen and got out the cookbook. I had started to put the lasagna together when the phone rang. I guessed it was Steph.

"Hi. I final—"

"Kelly!" Mom broke in. "Where have you been? I tried to get you at Stephie's and you'd already left."

"Mom, what's wrong? Is it Allyson?"

"Yes, I rushed her to the hospital. We'll be home in a little while."

"Is she all right?"

"She has some kind of infection. She has to go on antibiotics. I probably got overly concerned about her heart. More important, though, her blood pressure skyrocketed. Dr. Metzger says it's a good thing Allyson is having the transplant right away, before her arteries are permanently affected by the high blood pressure."

"Mom, wait, there's something I really have to—"

The phone connection was bad, and I guess she didn't hear me. She went on. "Because of Allyson's high blood pressure, she can't stay on dialysis too much longer."

Stunned, I hardly heard Mom tell me to go ahead with dinner.

"Your dad should get there soon, too," she was saying.

"Okay," I said numbly.

My mind was in a whirl and my heart was in my throat. I sat down on a stool and leaned my head on the counter. *What should I do now? How could I tell Allyson I'd changed my mind?*

In a daze, I finished making the lasagna and put it in the oven. Over and over, Mom's words kept echoing through my mind: *she can't stay on dialysis too much longer.* That meant Allyson couldn't go on the waiting list for a kidney. She could die before a kidney became available for her.

When I heard a car drive into the driveway, I hurried to the door. Coming up the walk, Allyson was leaning on Mom. I had never seen her look worse than she did then. She looked almost too weak to walk.

"Are you okay?" I asked, getting on the other side and helping Ally into the house.

"Not so great," she said with a weak smile. "I think I'll go right to bed."

Mom and I helped her into her nightgown. I was shocked to see how thin my sister was. The dark circles under her eyes looked even darker against her pasty white skin. Her eyes looked glassy and blank.

When Ally was settled in bed, Mom told

her, "I'll go fix you something to eat. Anything special you'd like?"

"Nothing, Mom. I just want to rest. I'm so tired."

After Mom left, I sat on the edge of the bed looking at Ally. And suddenly a rush of love swept over me. Somehow, I knew right then my sister meant more to me than anybody in the world. I knew I was the only one who could help her. If I didn't, then nobody could. And if she died, I knew it would be the worst thing in the world. Looking at her now, the way she looked so helpless and alone, all my doubts and fears melted away. I knew I couldn't let her down.

Before, I'd wanted to do something important. I saw the transplant as as way of proving to everybody that I was important, that I could be responsible. Now, all I could think about was Ally. Ally, my big sister who'd done so much for me, needed my help. She needed something that only I could give her.

I put my hand over hers. "Ally," I whispered, "you're going to feel lots better as soon as you get the transplant. I promise."

But she didn't hear me. She was sound asleep.

Ten

EVER since Christmas morning when Brian found out I planned to give Allyson one of my kidneys, he had never once brought up the subject. So I never mentioned it, either. When we were at the center, he'd usually ask how Allyson was doing. But he never came around our house much anymore, so I didn't know if he still had a crush on her.

I had just finished a race, and I'd had my fastest time ever. *Pretty soon I'll have a ribbon of my own to put in a shadow box frame,* I thought. *Just like Allyson's.*

"Great riding, Kelly," Brian said, coming up behind me as I was walking Sidekick to cool him down. "I'm betting on you to win the competition next week."

Right, if I even *got* to compete. Allyson's infection had delayed the transplant. The doctors planned to do the operations the minute she was okay again. "I sure hope so,"

I said. "I've been working hard enough."

"My parents are positive all of us are going to win," added Brian. "They're throwing a big party when we get back from Fresno. You're invited," he said without looking at me.

I didn't want to tell him I might be in the hospital. "Thanks, but I may be busy. If I can, I'll be there."

"Sure," he said coldly. "Well, I'm going to see how Steph's doing." He took off at a run.

"Brian, wait. I want..." What was the use? I didn't understand why he was so against the transplant. And it looked like I never would.

* * * * *

My timing has always been lousy. Mom said I was born two weeks later than she and the doctor expected. I miss the bus to school a lot. I'm late for classes. So, I shouldn't have been surprised when I found out that the timing for the operations was the worst time possible. I had to be at the hospital the very same day Brian and Steph and the others from our club were going to the competition in Fresno.

Allyson had to go to the hospital a couple of days before the operations for a complete physical. The social worker talked to both of us again. This time I had no doubts at all.

Oh, sure I was still a little scared. I mean, who wouldn't be? I don't even like going to the dentist.

The night before Ally went to the hospital, the whole family was in the living room. Grandma Allyson and Aunt Fran had flown down from San Francisco. Keith had just gone home, promising Allyson he'd visit her every day in the hospital.

I envied her. My two best friends would be out of town.

"That's a nice young man," Aunt Fran said to Allyson. "I expect we'll be hearing wedding bells one of these days."

Grandma Allyson shook her head. "Fran, you're a hopeless romantic. Ally's too young to get married."

"We both want to go to college," Allyson said quickly, before they could get into a long argument over marriage. "We're just good friends."

Sure, I thought. *So were Romeo and Juliet.*

"Well, I'm really tired," Ally said after a little while. "If nobody minds, I think I'll go to bed."

I figured she'd have a hard time going to sleep. I was already wired, and I didn't have to go to the hospital for two more days. "I'm pretty tired, too," I said yawning. "Ally, would you mind if I slept in your room tonight?"

"I'd like that," she said. "Just promise you won't snore."

"What do you mean? I don't snore—" I began, then saw her grinning. "Okay, I promise."

As we kissed everybody goodnight, Mom said to me, "Kelly, don't you keep your sister awake with your talking. She needs her rest."

"Don't worry," Ally said. "If she talks too much, I'll shove a pillow over her face!"

Ally had been kidding around all evening, but I think she was just covering up how she really felt. Scared. Really scared.

Neither of us said much as we got ready for bed. I didn't know if I ought to bring up the subject that was on our minds or not. I folded back the yellow quilted spread on her other twin bed and climbed in. She stood in front of the dialysis machine next to her bed, just staring at it.

"What's wrong, Ally? Don't tell me you're going to miss the 'Monster'?"

She laughed softly. "No way. I was just thinking how nice it'll be not to get tired all the time, to feel *normal* again."

She switched off the light. I could just barely see her face from the moonlight streaming through the white curtains.

"Kelly?" Her voice sounded hesitant, uncertain. I had a feeling she was going to bring up the subject. "Do you think I've made the right decision? What if your kidney doesn't work for me? Maybe Aunt Fran is right. Maybe transplants *are* wrong."

"How can anything be wrong that makes people's lives better? Look how many lives are saved?"

"Kell, you don't seem scared at all. I'm terrified."

I came really close to telling her that I'd almost backed out. "I'm scared, too," I said softly.

I got out of bed and climbed in beside her, just the way I used to do when I was little. "Remember when I used to get in your bed when I'd had a nightmare?"

"I sure do. You always had the *coldest* feet." She chuckled. "Whenever we had a thunderstorm, you'd jump in here like you'd been shot out of a cannon."

"You never once told me to get lost," I reminded her. "You always made me feel better."

"That's what big sisters are for."

"Well, for the first time, this little sister gets to help you."

"Giving your kidney is a lot bigger deal than putting up with a scared little kid with cold feet." She gave me a playful push and I almost fell off the bed. "Have you noticed how much

106

narrower this bed is than it used to be?"

I gave her a push back. "It couldn't be that we're a lot bigger now, could it?"

"Remember the pillow fights we used to have?" she asked.

"Yeah," I said, thinking of all the fun we'd had together. "Remember how Mom got disgusted and took away all the feather pillows and bought us foam rubber ones."

"How about that time we got in a fight with the neighbor kids' water pistols?" She giggled. "You put red food coloring in yours."

"Yes, but you weren't satisfied with water pistols," I said. "You got a bottle of soda, shook it up, and aimed it at me as I headed for the door. Remember?"

"Do I remember?" She groaned. "If only Dad hadn't picked that moment to come to see what all the yelling was about. I don't think he's ever forgiven me for that black eye he got."

We both burst out laughing. "Dad told everybody that Mom socked him," I said.

"I guess he figured nobody would believe he'd run into a door." She choked, trying not to laugh. "I don't think Dad thought it was so funny."

"We've had a lot of good times," I said, and then we were quiet. Some of my friends don't get along with their brothers or sisters. Maybe

Ally and I are just lucky. I was really going to miss her when she went off to college.

We talked about old times for a while, then Allyson said softly, "Thanks, Kelly. You've made me feel better tonight. If you don't mind, though, I'd kind of like to be by myself now."

"I know," I said, making a joke out of it. "It's my cold feet."

"Right."

I climbed out of her bed. "Are you sure you're okay?"

"I am now." She reached her arms up and we hugged. She clung to me for a minute, then gently pushed me away. "I still have a few butterflies, but I'm better now."

"Did you know the original name for butterflies was *flutterbies?*"

"You and your trivia are going to drive me crazy," she said with a laugh. "I think I *will* stuff a pillow over your face!"

"I'm outta here," I said. At the door, I turned back. "If *you* have a nightmare or—or anything—you know where to find me."

"I know," she said, almost in a whisper. "Goodnight, little sister."

I closed the door softly behind me. Little sister? Tonight I felt like the older sister.

Eleven

ALLY went to the hospital the next day for the operation. A few days later, the afternoon before Stephie and Brian left for the competition in Fresno, I called Steph.

"I just wanted to wish you good luck in the competition," I said. "But I know you won't need luck. You're good."

"Thanks, Kell. I'm sure sorry you'll be in the hospital. You've worked so hard."

"I'll survive," I said, trying to hide how much I wanted to be with them.

"I guess you're all packed and ready to go to the hospital tonight."

"Yeah, right after dinner," I said. "The waiting has been driving me nuts. I feel as if my life's been on hold the last few weeks."

"Are you scared, Kell?"

"Yeah, I get kind of queasy whenever I think about tomorrow," I admitted.

"Any more doubts about going through with

it?" she asked in a low voice.

"No. I just want to get it over with," I said, trying to sound cheerful. "I didn't call to talk about me. Have fun and do great in Fresno."

"Thanks, Kelly. Everything's going to go well for you and Allyson. I just know it will. I'll be thinking about you the whole time."

"Well, I guess I'll call Brian and wish him luck, too."

She hesitated a second. Then she said, "Umm, he's—uh—here."

"Oh?" I couldn't hide my surprise.

"We're going over last minute plans," she said quickly.

"Oh," I said again. "Sure—plans."

"You can talk to him, Kell. He's standing right here."

"It's Kelly," I heard her whisper. Then she said something that was too muffled for me to hear.

"Hi," Brian said. "Listen, I can't talk right now, but you try to think positive and get well right away. You hear?"

"Sure. Call me when you guys get back," I said. "I want to know how you both did."

"We will." I thought he sounded impatient to hang up. "Sorry to cut this short, Kell, but we have a lot to do yet."

Stephie broke in. "Hang in there, Kelly."

"See you..." My words trailed off. I slowly

hung up the phone. Weird. Stephie had acted strangely. I figured it was because she felt guilty about going off to Fresno. So much for those TV and newspaper stories about me.

Okay, Kelly, I told myself. Stop feeling sorry for yourself. It's just lousy timing.

* * * * *

Early the next morning Allyson and I were wheeled on gurneys to the surgical holding room. Mom and Dad kissed us both. Keith squeezed my hand, then kissed Allyson. They were all trying not to look worried.

"This is going to be a piece of cake," I told them. I tried to snap my fingers. But they were so sweaty I couldn't do it.

Some of my bravery—a lot of it, in fact— melted away as the heavy doors swung shut and closed them out. For some reason, I guess I'd thought Mom and Dad would be in surgery with us. But we left them behind, and it felt like they were a million miles away.

My heart was beating like a drummer in a heavy metal band. Attendants wheeled us into a large room where a lot of other patients were waiting for operations. "Put me right beside my sister," I told a nurse. "We have to stay together."

Allyson hardly said a word. We were both

a little groggy from the sedative the nurse had given us to make us calm. "Are you scared?" I whispered to Allyson.

"A little," she said. Her voice sounded trembly. "I just want to close my eyes, go to sleep, and get it over with."

"Not me." I rose up so that I could look around. "I sort of wish I could stay awake and watch what's going on. Maybe I'll become a transplant surgeon."

"I hope we're doing the right thing, Kell," she said softly. You can still back out, you know."

"No way, Sis. We're in this together."

I wanted to take her mind off the operation. I gave her a sly grin. "But can I borrow your new yellow blouse when we get home?"

"What a blackmailer!" She laughed. "You can borrow anything I have—if you loan me a kidney." We both laughed together.

Two anesthetists came in then to talk to us. I hardly recognized Dr. Whitman in his green scrubs. He'd worn a suit last night when he came to see me in my hospital room.

"How come we have different ones?" I asked Dr. Whitman. I always have trouble saying the word *anesthetist.*

"You and Allyson will be in different surgical rooms," Dr. Whitman said.

I hadn't realized that either. "But we'll be

in the same room afterwards, won't we?"

He shook his head. "No. Your sister has to have special attention."

"I know," I said. "ICU. Intensive Care Unit. She has to be monitored. Did I tell you I'm going to be a doctor?"

He smiled. "Kelly, everybody in the hospital knows it."

I asked some more questions while he was doing things to my arm. I started to get sleepy, and I reached out for Allyson's hand. "You're going to be okay from now on," I told her.

"I'll never forget what you're doing for me, Kell..." Her voice drifted off.

* * * * *

The next thing I remember is someone calling my name. "Wake up, Kelly."

"I'm too sleepy," I mumbled. "Can I stay home from school today?"

"Kelly, sweetheart, we're right here."

I was lying on my right side on a bed in my hospital room. My left side and back hurt so much I didn't want to move a muscle. *Hey, what's wrong with me?* Then I remembered. I was short one kidney. I tried to focus my eyes. I saw Mom and Dad.

"Ally!" I croaked. My throat hurt when I tried to swallow.

"You had a tube in your throat," Mom said gently. "It'll feel sore for a while."

"Is Allyson all right?"

"The doctor said the operation went well," Dad said. "She hasn't awakened yet."

"You're sure she's okay? Shouldn't you be with her?"

"Her nurse will call us as soon as she comes out of the anesthetic," Mom said.

"How soon can I see her?" I asked. I wanted to see for myself that she was really okay.

"Maybe tomorrow. Right now, though, there are two people who've been waiting for hours to see you."

"Who? Grandma and Aunt Fran?"

"No. They'll be here later," Mom said, then looked at Dad with a funny little smile. "Your brother and sister got permission to come in for a minute. We'll be right outside."

"Brother? Sister?" I was still woozy, but not *that* woozy. "But I don't have—" I stopped as Stephie and Brian walked into the room. For once in my life I was totally speechless.

"Close your mouth," Brian said. "Or else the nurses won't believe that we're your brother and sister."

"I don't think they did, anyhow," Stephie said with a laugh. "How do you feel, Kell?"

"Okay," I lied. I was really hurting a lot. "Of course I'll never be able to play pro football,"

I kidded. "But what are you guys doing here? Was the competition canceled?"

Stephie pretended to look mad. "You didn't think we'd go off and leave you at a time like this, did you?"

"But...but...what about the team?"

"Coach found two subs to take our places. We wouldn't have done very well, anyhow," Brian said. "We were too worried about you."

So that's why they'd acted so strangely last night. "You two are sure sneaky. You shouldn't have done it, but boy, I'm glad you guys are here." Then I remembered something. "Brian, what about the party your parents were throwing after the competition?"

He shrugged it off. "It wouldn't have been a party without you. We can just have it later."

Stephie looked around the room. "This is great. Isn't anyone using the other bed?"

"I guess not." I tried to laugh. But it hurt too much. I settled for a smile. "Want to sleep over?"

"They told us we could only stay a minute now," Brian said. "We'll be back tomorrow as soon as they'll let us in."

"I'm glad you're okay," Stephie said softly and touched my arm. "Believe me, I was really worried."

"So was I," said Brian.

They both waved good-bye. As I watched

them leave, I had a lump in my sore throat about the size of a watermelon. And it wasn't from the tube either. Stephie was the best friend in the world, and Brian...well, Brian had really seemed concerned about me.

* * * * *

The rest of the day, I slept a lot from the pain shots. That night the nurse made me get up and sit in a chair for a few minutes. That was agony, but it's supposed to help you heal faster to get up and move around.

When the nurse let me see Ally the next day, I had to put on a coat and mask, and even paper slippers, so she wouldn't get an infection. Her eyes were closed and for a minute, my heart did a flip-flop. *Is she okay?* Then she opened her eyes and smiled at me. For a minute there, I'd thought the worst.

Relieved, I asked, "How're you doing, Ally?"

She reached for my hand. "I feel better already." Then she whispered, "I know it doesn't sound like a big deal, but I can actually go to the bathroom again!"

"Just don't get too rambunctious, as Aunt Fran always says. After all, you have to take care of *my* kidney. Or else I might ask for it back!" I grinned to let her know I was kidding.

"I'll guard it with my life." Her face turned

serious. "How about you, Kell? Are you hurting a lot?"

"It's not too bad." I didn't feel like telling her the truth. I knew she had it worse.

"Kelly, there's no way I can ever pay you back."

"Sure you can," I joked. "You can give me your yellow blouse. No, honestly, Sis, all I want is for you to feel good again. That's the best way you can pay me back."

We talked for a while longer about all the things we were going to do when we got home. Then Mom came in.

"Kelly, honey, I think you'd better go back to your room. Allyson needs to rest and so do you."

"As soon as they let me walk that far, I'll come visit you," Ally said.

Mom and the nurse helped me back to my room.

"I know you and Dad want to be with Ally as much as you can," I said. "Why don't you go back and visit her?"

"Are you trying to get rid of me?" she asked, pretending to be hurt as we walked down the long hall.

"You know I'm not, but I'm okay. I have some books and magazines, and I can watch TV. I won't get lonesome. Stephie and Brian said they'd be here today. I can't believe they gave up the competition for me."

"You're very lucky to have such good friends."

"I know."

When we got to the door of my room, Mom said, "I think I will go back to see how Allyson is doing."

Although it had been my idea, I felt a little let down. Maybe I would get a little lonely. "Uh, sure, Mom. I'll see you later."

When I walked into my room, I thought I was in the wrong one. It was filled with balloons and flowers, and even a tree made of get-well cards. The curtain was pulled around the other bed. But I knew I was in the right room when I saw the sign. Pinned on the curtain was a huge computer-printed banner that said KELLY REED IS THE GREAT-EST!

"Hey, what's going on?" I whispered. Then I noticed two pairs of feet sticking out from under the curtain. "Okay," I said. "Come out, come out, whoever you are."

Grinning like a couple of idiots, Stephie and Brian came out from behind the curtain. I just kept shaking my head as I looked around the room.

"Do you like it?" Brian asked proudly.

"I love it! It's you two who are the greatest, though." I sank down on my bed. "I didn't think I was gone long enough for you to do all this."

"Your mother would have kept you away if we'd needed more time," Stephie said. "Some of the flowers and cards are from your other friends. They'll take turns coming to see you."

Brian gave me a crossword puzzle book, a bag of my favorite malted milk balls, and a red rose from his garden. Stephie brought me some new makeup I'd been wanting.

"I feel like a queen or something," I said. I waved my hand around, looking at all the things they'd brought. "This is terrific. If I'd known I'd get this much attention, I'd have found some excuse to go to the hospital before now. Maybe I'll have another operation."

I started to swing my legs up on the bed, and a pain shot through my side and back. "Ow! On the other hand, I think I'll wait a while."

My nurse came in to take my temperature.

"Maybe we should go," Stephie said. "You look tired."

I nodded. As soon as the nurse took the thermometer out of my mouth, I said, "Yeah, I guess maybe I am. You'll come back tomorrow, won't you?"

"Every day," Steph said. "And we have another surprise for you when you're stronger."

"What is it?"

"Sorry. We have to go," she said, ignoring my question.

"Now don't be so impatient," said Brian in a teasing way. "We'll be back."

As they left, I called, "Thanks, guys—for everything."

I had another surprise. That night when visiting hours were almost over, Mom came over to the bed. She looked down at me so long, I got a little scared.

"What's wrong, Mom? You look—funny."

"I just wanted you to know how proud your father and I are."

Then Dad took something out of a bag. "This is for you, Kelly," he said. He handed me a beautiful shadow box. Inside it was a blue ribbon. On it in little yellow letters were the words, *Best daughter in the fourteen-year-old age group.*

"You remembered! I love it. I love it." I started to cry, then I started to laugh. Then I winced from the pain in my side. "Ooh, that hurts."

"Here, I'll put it over on the table by your flowers," Mom said.

"No, I want to hold it for a while. Ally gave me her medal, but this is the first prize I've ever won myself!"

I was still smiling at my ribbon when the nurse came in to get me settled for the night.

Twelve

I was luckier than Ally. She couldn't have much company or even flowers in her room. But a lot of my friends from school and the Boots and Saddle Club came to see me. Aunt Fran and Grandma each gave me twenty-five dollars to buy whatever I wanted when I got out of the hospital. I felt like I could get used to all that attention.

Brian usually came to the hospital with Stephie. The afternoon of my fourth day, I was surprised to see him walk in alone. He had a bouquet of roses. "Mom just picked these," he said, looking kind of embarrassed. "She thought you'd enjoy them."

"Thanks," I said. "I mean, thank your mother." He stood by the door like a rabbit ready to run from a coyote.

"Come on in and pull up a chair. Better yet, go for a walk with me."

"Should you do that?" he asked. "Doesn't

it hurt to walk around?"

"Sure, but not too much. I've been walking since the day after surgery. If you'll go out in the hall for a minute, I'll get on my robe. These crazy hospital gowns are the pits."

Looking even more embarrassed, he ducked out into the hall. I'd never seen him like that before. I got into my robe and slippers, trying to ignore the pain. It still hurt to cough or bend over. Coughing was really important. The nurse made me do it so my lungs wouldn't fill up with fluid. If I didn't cough, I might get pneumonia. I met Brian in the hall. We walked slowly down the corridor.

"Have you been in to see Allyson yet?" I asked.

"No." He grinned sheepishly. "The nurses in ICU didn't buy the brother bit."

"I'm sorry. I know how much you must want to see her."

He gave me a funny look. "Well, sure," he said.

"There's something I've wanted to ask you, Brian."

"Shoot."

I stopped walking and turned to face him. "How come you were so against the whole transplant idea when you knew how much it would help Allyson?"

"I-I wasn't against the transplant."

122

"But you said—"

"I was just afraid about *you* giving her *your* kidney," he blurted. He wasn't looking at me. "I was wor—I mean, all your friends were worried about you. Why do you think Steph and I didn't go to Fresno?"

Hey, he likes me. He really must like me, I thought. "That was great. I'll never forget that," I said softly.

"Aw, it was nothing. Hey, did you know a cockroach can live for weeks with its head cut off?"

Boy, when he changed a subject, he *changed* a subject!

"No," I answered. "Did you know that if you get even a moderately severe sunburn, it takes your damaged blood vessels from four to fifteen months to get back to normal?"

We were sharing trivia when a patient came out of one of the rooms. He looked familiar. We both stopped and stared at each other for a second. "I've got it," he finally said. "You were at the dialysis center."

"Tom?" His face looked as if he'd been stuffing walnuts in his cheeks. "You were waiting for a kidney. Did your beeper ever go off?"

"Yep. I had a transplant a month or so after I saw you. I'm surprised you recognized me. The medication gave me these chipmunk cheeks and made me put on weight."

I nodded toward his hospital room. "I hope it went okay."

"I had a rejection episode. I was pretty dumb. I felt so good I eased up on my medication. I thought I was going to lose my new kidney, but I'm fine now. I'm going home tomorrow."

"That's great." Then I remembered my manners. I introduced him to Brian.

"I guess I'd better be going," Brian said. "I'll be back this evening." Before I could say anything, he took off.

I guess Tom saw my disappointment. "I'm sorry I scared off your boyfriend," he said after Brian had left.

"Oh, he's not my boyfriend," I said quickly.

"Oh?" Tom gave me the same kind of grin as Ally had when we'd talked about Brian.

Hmm. Could it be that maybe they were right? I'd gotten so used to thinking that Brian liked Allyson. The habit was hard to break.

"I didn't mean to embarrass you," Tom said, then frowned. "You look tired. Why don't we sit down for a while?"

We walked over to one of the little sitting areas. I carefully sat down on a low couch. "You're right," I said with a sigh. "I am tired."

"But what are you here for?" he asked. "I hope it's nothing serious."

"Oh, it's serious. But it's wonderful, too. I

just gave one of my kidneys to my sister."

"Wow!" Tom cried. "That's great. She'll have much less chance of rejection since you're her sister. Be sure and tell her that even though she doesn't like the side effects, she should take the medication as prescribed."

I nodded. "The doctors warned her about that."

"Believe me," Tom answered. "Even with the worst side effects, it's worth it to have the kidney. I've felt a hundred percent better. I feel as if I've been given a new life."

What Tom said made me even more glad I'd given Ally my kidney than I had been before. I knew then I had done the right thing.

"Your family must be very proud of you," he said.

"It's no big deal," I said, trying not to burst my hospital gown from feelings of pride. "I told the social worker that I'd go into a burning building to save my sister. The operation was a whole lot easier than that would be!"

"I just hope more people start signing donor cards so when they die, their organs can save lives. If there were more organs available, people like you wouldn't ever have to give up a kidney." He gave me a sheepish smile. "Hey, I'm sorry. I get carried away sometimes."

He looked at the big clock on the wall. "A friend's coming to visit. I'd better get back to my room. It's been nice talking to you, Kelly."

"Me, too," I said, and meant it. He'd made me feel great. "I hope you hang on to that kidney."

"The same goes for your sister. Kelly, there's one tip I'll give you," he added. "Don't treat your sister like an invalid. When I came home, everybody acted as if I were a ghost. Try not to make her feel 'different.' Do you know what I mean?"

"I sure do. Thanks."

"One more thing, Kelly. If things get rough, just remember this. You gave your sister the gift of life."

The gift of life. He was right. No matter what happened, even if Ally's body rejected my kidney, I knew I'd never, ever regret my decision. I gave Ally the gift of life.

* * * * *

On the fifth day, Allyson moved into my room. I had to un-pin my banner from the curtain and tape it to the wall. "This is great," Ally said, looking around at the balloons and flowers.

Of course, some of the balloons had lost air, and the flowers had started to wilt. But I couldn't bear to throw anything out. "I'll push my stuff aside so you'll have room for your flowers," I said. "The volunteer brought a lot of flowers for you this morning."

"We look like a florist shop," she answered, smelling a bouquet of long-stemmed yellow roses that must have cost Keith a fortune.

The nurse helped her get settled. Allyson looked great, better than I'd seen her look in months.

"I'm glad they let me move in here, Kell."

"Me, too." It was weird, but I wanted her near so I could sort of keep an eye on her. "But I get first choice on the TV shows."

"Okay, but you have to promise not to ask me any trivia questions."

"Okay. It's a deal."

Before she even finished putting her things away, her friends started showing up. They took all the chairs and there wasn't room for any of my friends. I didn't say anything, though. Having visitors made Ally look so happy.

Then the next day I found out what Stephie meant when she said there was an even bigger surprise coming. She came through on her promise to ask the newspaper to do a story on Allyson and me. Stephie helped me fix my hair and makeup before the reporter and photographer arrived.

The interview didn't go exactly the way I'd expected, though. The reporter asked Ally most of the questions. The photographer took a lot of pictures of Ally alone, then a few of us together. Stephie moved out of the way, looking upset about something. "Aren't you going to take a picture of Kelly's banner?" she asked the photographer.

The photographer glanced at it. "I'm afraid it wouldn't show up," he said and took another shot of Allyson.

Stephie walked out of the room. I followed her. "Hey, Steph, what's wrong?"

"I set this up so they'd do a story on you and the incredibly wonderful thing you did for your sister."

"I'm sorry you're disappointed, Steph, but Ally's the one who had the transplant."

"I'm not thinking about me, Kell. They hardly even talked to you. It's not fair to *you!*" she said angrily.

"Oh, I don't mind," I said, although I *was* feeling kind of left out.

"Well, I still think the story should be about you." She snapped her fingers. "Wait! I know. I'll write a story for our school paper."

I grinned. "Stephanie Miller, you just want to say your best friend is a celebrity."

She grinned back.

* * * * *

After a week in the hospital, Allyson and I were both anxious to get home. The doctors said they were planning to release us in a few days. I couldn't wait, and neither could Ally!

I had decided to keep a close eye on Ally for any signs of flu-like symptoms. They could mean that she was starting to reject my kidney. One day, while we were eating breakfast in our hospital room, she sneezed.

"Ally, are you all right?" I asked.

"Listen, you worrywart, you're worse than Mom and Dad. I just sprinkled pepper on my egg. Pepper always makes me sneeze."

"I can't help it, Ally. I do worry about you."

"I'll tell you if I start to feel bad," she said. "Actually, my only problem right now is that I can't go to the bathroom and my stomach's a little swollen up."

I dropped my spoon on the tray. "You'd better tell the nurse. That doesn't sound good to me."

"Thank you, Dr. Kelly Reed," she said in a mocking tone of voice. "The nurses keep track of it, you know."

"Okay, but I still think you should ask them about it."

She was right about the nurses keeping track of her output of urine. That afternoon they took her for some tests, a renal scan and an ultrasound, a nurse said. After Ally had been gone for a few hours, I asked the nurse what was wrong. She said Dr. Metzger would tell us.

Just then Mom and Dad came hurrying into the room.

"Where is Allyson?" Dad asked me. "Dr. Metzger called us."

"They took her for some tests," I said anxiously. "Did the doctor tell you what's wrong?"

"No," Mom answered. "But he should be here soon."

Mom sat down. I noticed she kept twisting the handle of her purse. Dad paced across the room like a lion in a cage at the zoo. I knew they were plenty worried when Mom added, "We called Grandma Allyson and Aunt Fran. They'll be here in a few hours."

Oh, no! Ice settled in my stomach. I knew they wouldn't have called Grandma and Aunt Fran unless they were afraid Ally might—I pushed the thought away. It was too horrible to even think about!

Dr. Metzger didn't show up for a couple more hours. But we were all so nervous and frightened it seemed like weeks.

"Sorry I'm late," he apologized. "One of my young patients was killed in a motorcycle accident. I couldn't get in touch with his parents for permission to save his organs." He sighed and shook his head. "Such a waste. He could have given the gift of life."

The nurse wheeled Ally in a wheelchair into the room. Allyson looked numb. "What's wrong with me, Dr. Metzger?" she cried. "Why did I have to have more tests?"

"Allyson, I'm afraid we have a little problem," he said without emotion. "We're going to have to take you back to surgery."

Ally just stared at him with frightened eyes. *Surgery?* What was going on? She was supposed to be okay now that she had my kidney. A chill ran down my back.

Mom's voice shook as she asked, "Is Allyson rejecting the kidney?"

"We're afraid there's some damage to the drainage tube from the kidney to the bladder. The tissue and the blood supply can die."

An icy hand seemed to grab my heart and suddenly I couldn't breathe.

Allyson kept shaking her head. "I don't understand. I thought I was all right." She was in tears. "Nobody told me this might happen. Am I—" Allyson choked. "Am I going to die?"

"You're in good hands, Allyson," the doctor said. "Dr. Evans is one of the best surgeons in California."

But he hadn't answered Ally's question. It echoed in my ears and the hallways of the huge hospital. But no answer came back.

Was she going to die?

131

Thirteen

THE nurses quickly got Allyson ready to go to surgery. Mom and Dad left for a minute to sign some papers. When Ally and I were alone for a minute, she clutched my hand. "I'm more scared than I was for the transplant," she said in a tiny, frightened voice, almost a whisper.

I was scared, too, but I tried to hide it. "You're going to be fine. Didn't Dr. Metzger say you had one of the best surgeons in California?"

But Ally saw right through me. "Don't try to con me, Kelly," she said. "I can tell by your eyes that you're afraid, too."

I crossed my eyes, desperately trying to kid her out of it. "How can you tell anything by these eyes?" I asked in a goofy voice.

But I saw the pain and fear in her face and knew this was no time to joke around. "Yeah,

I'm scared, Sis. I'm really scared." I couldn't even dare to think about what could happen. But then Ally mentioned what I was most afraid of.

In a hushed voice, she said, "If I die, I want you to know—"

"Ally, you aren't going to die!" I cried. "You can't die!"

She put her hand over my lips. "Shh. I want you to know how much I love you, Little Sister." She gave me a weak little smile. "And, Kell, the yellow blouse is yours."

My throat got so tight I could hardly speak. "I don't want the blouse, Ally. I want you." Tears started streaming down my face and sobs shook my whole body. "Anyway, I look awful in yellow."

Then Ally was comforting me. "Don't cry, Kelly Belly. Please don't cry."

We clung to each other for a minute, then the nurses came to take her to surgery. *No, something inside me cried out. Don't take her away from me! You can't take her away!*

Mom and Dad returned just as they were wheeling Ally out. Allyson grabbed their hands. "I'm glad you got back in time."

"We called Keith," Mom told her. "He'll be here soon."

I slipped into my robe and slippers and

started to follow them.

"Honey," Mom said to me, "I think you'd better wait here. It could be a long time."

I knew I'd go crazy alone in my room. "Please, let me stay with you."

"You're still recuperat—"

"I'll be going home in a few days. I'm not sick. *Please*," I begged. "Please don't leave me here alone!"

"We'll ask the nurse."

The nurse said I could go in a wheelchair to the waiting room for an hour. At the door to the surgery room, we all kissed Ally. I whispered to her, "I love you, Sis."

She gave my hand a little squeeze. But her eyes were looking off somewhere else and I don't even think she saw us anymore. She seemed to be off in her own world. And none of us could follow her there.

Is this the last time I'll ever see her? I tried not to think about it, but the thought kept pushing its way into my mind, taking over my thoughts like a huge, evil black bird blotting out the sky. *Are they taking her away forever?*

She's not going to die. She's not going to die. She's not going to die...

The heavy doors swung shut. Behind them was Ally. My sister. Would I ever see her again?

*　*　*　*　*

Keith, Stephie, and Brian were in the surgery waiting room by the time we got there. Keith rushed up to Mom and Dad.

"I got your message. What's wrong?" Keith's voice was panicky and his face was white as a ghost. "Is she rejecting the kidney? What's going on?"

Dad explained about the damaged drainage tube. "It's a long operation. Not only could she lose the kidney, but we could lose—" Dad stopped and turned quickly away.

Mom gently touched Keith's shoulder. "Allyson's strong, Keith. We have to be strong, too."

No one spoke for a while. We were all alone with our thoughts. I half-listened to the talk show on the TV until I couldn't bear it anymore. It almost drove me crazy to think that it was just a normal day for everyone else. There were people all over the country watching the stupid talk show about who should do the housework, the husband or the wife.

What did I care who did the dumb housework?! Didn't that talk show host know that my sister was in the operating room fighting for her life while he blabbed on and on about vacuuming and dusting?!?

Finally, I blurted out, "I think it's harder to wait for someone to get out of surgery than it is to *have* an operation!"

Stephie was sitting on a couch next to my wheelchair. "I know," she said. "Brian and I waited here for three hours last week."

"So, how did you know Ally had to go back to surgery?" I asked.

"Brian and I came to visit you. The nurse told us where you were."

We talked for a while about unimportant things like the weather and having to go back to school in June. Then we got quiet again and listened to some of the other people who were waiting for someone to get out of surgery. Sometimes I stared at the TV, only now it was some ridiculous soap opera about somebody being kidnapped by animal-rights terrorists. *That's not real life,* I thought. *Real life is here, in this waiting room, in the operating room where Ally is.*

I kept watching the clock. The hands seemed to be stuck. We'd only been waiting 45 minutes, but it seemed like forever. Then all of a sudden it was time for me to go back upstairs. "Thanks for being here," I said to Steph and Brian.

"I'm going with you," Stephie said without any hesitation.

136

"Me, too," Brian said. "I don't want you to be alone." He unlocked the brake on the wheelchair. "I'll drive."

I told Mom and Dad I was going. "Maybe the nurse will let me come back later."

"If you can't," Mom said, "we'll let you know as soon as we hear anything." She turned to Brian and Steph. "Thanks for being with Kelly today."

I don't know what I would have done if I'd had to go back up to my room and wait there alone. At lunchtime, Brian got sandwiches from one of the snack machines. I hardly touched a thing on my tray.

"Are you okay, Kelly?" Brian asked.

"I'm fine," I muttered.

"You're not a very good liar," he said.

"Okay," I said angrily. "So what if I'm not all right? It's just not fair that all this has to happen to Ally. She's been...through enough." I wandered over to the door. "What if..., what if she...dies?" Tears filled my eyes again. It was all so unfair. One person shouldn't have to suffer so much!

Stephie came over to my side. "Allyson's young. She's a fighter."

At least she didn't say, *Everything's going to be all right.* I think I would have screamed if I had heard that one more time.

137

"I know how serious this is," I said. "I'm so afraid..."

Brian came over and put his arm around me. "Thinking the worst isn't going to help. Come on, let's play a game, to take our minds off it. I brought my Rummy Cube."

"M-maybe you're right," I said between sniffs.

He set up the tiles and we tried to play. I just couldn't concentrate, and finally I couldn't stand it any longer. "I'm sorry guys," I said. "I just have to go back downstairs."

I got permission from the nurse to go to the waiting room for another hour. When we got there, I saw that Mom and Dad looked tired.

"Have you heard anything?" I asked them.

Dad shook his head. "The doctor will come and tell us as soon as he's through."

"But it's been such a long time!" I cried. "Something must have gone wrong!"

Suddenly, I couldn't breathe. I felt like I had to get away from there—fast. I swung my wheelchair around, knocking over a magazine stand, and started out to the corridor. I saw Grandma and Aunt Fran hurrying toward me.

"Kelly," Grandma said, all out of breath, "is Allyson still in surgery?"

"I don't know why it's taking so long," I cried.

They went right into the waiting room. I took some deep breaths, trying to get a hold of myself, and then went back in, too.

"Tell us about Allyson," Aunt Fran was saying. "Have you had any word?"

Dad shook his head. "Nothing."

"I knew the transplant was a mistake," Aunt Fran muttered. "I just wish you'd all listened to me."

Grandma glared at her. "If you're going to be such a voice of doom, Fran, you should have stayed in San Francisco."

"I'm just stating the facts. Allyson should never have had a transplant."

"It was her decision, Aunt Fran," I said quietly.

"She's not even old enough to vote. She's too young to make a life-and-death decision."

Before anybody could answer, the doctor suddenly came into the room. We all stared at him. I tried to tell by his face whether he had good or bad news. I held my breath. *Please, let her be all right. Please let Ally be okay.*

"Is she all right?" Mom asked finally, her voice trembling. Dad put his arm around her waist.

"Allyson is in recovery." The doctor's voice sounded tired. "The surgery went well.

Allyson is in stable condition."

I let out my held breath. I think everyone else did, too. I blinked, trying hard not to cry. But it was no use. I couldn't hold back the tears. *Thank you, God. Thank you.*

"Were you able to save the kidney?" Mom asked.

"We still have to deal with the possibility of rejection, but for right now she's doing as well as can be expected."

I burst into sobs.

Mom put her arm around me. "Honey, are you all right? What's wrong?"

"I'm just crying because...I'm...so happy!"

*   *   *   *   *

When the nurses finally let us in to see Ally a few hours later, she gave us all a weak smile. "Hey, why does everybody look so sad?" she asked in a whispery voice. "I'm alive and kicking. Well, maybe not kicking," she added, "but I'm alive."

We all laughed, cutting the tension in the air.

Then Ally's face turned serious. "I forgot to tell you something before I went into surgery."

"Honey, don't try to talk now," Mom said.

"No, it's important. I still might have complications."

"You're going to be just fine," Grandma said.

"Mom, Dad, it's something you need to know."

Her voice was so weak that we had to gather around to hear her.

"If I die before I'm eighteen, I want you to give the doctors permission to use my organs."

"Allyson!" Aunt Fran cried. "You don't know what you're saying."

"Yes, I do know. Nobody knows it better than I do. If it hadn't been for Kelly, I might have died waiting for a kidney. I don't want someone else to die because there were no kidneys or livers."

Aunt Fran just kept shaking her head. "It's wrong," she said.

"It's not wrong!" I said. I was afraid Mom would scold me for talking back to my aunt. But she never said a word. I took Ally's hand. "That goes for me, too," I said. "How can giving the gift of life be wrong?"

Mom looked at Dad for a moment, then they both nodded. "I hope we never have to face that time," Mom said. "But if it means that much to you two—we'll do it."

Ally squeezed my hand. "Listen," she said

141

with a weak smile. "Kelly and I plan to live to a hundred. But just in case we don't—"

I finished the sentence for her. "We want to donate our organs to save someone else's life."

*   *   *   *   *

Allyson and I got off our horses and started to walk them through the woods. I patted Sidekick's neck and took his reins. Ally gave Airborne a lump of sugar. We watched as he took it neatly out of her hand.

We breathed in the the clear fall air and felt the warm sunshine on our skin. On such a beautiful day, the hospital and the operations felt like they were a million years ago, even though it had only been about five months. Since coming home from the hospital, we hadn't really talked too much about the transplant. It seemed like just having Ally back to normal, seeing her like her old self every day and knowing she was better, was enough. We didn't have to say how happy we were and all that. We both just knew.

I don't need to tell you how it felt to be out riding with Ally again. With her kidney troubles past, Ally was back to being the greatest sister a kid could ever have. But somehow, the operations had made us even closer. Knowing that there was a part of me inside her made us seem even more like sisters than we were before. No matter where we were, even if we grew up and lived a long way apart, that part of me would still be there with her, always. It was a good feeling.

"Hey, Kell," she asked after we had been resting by a stream for a few minutes, just enjoying the beautiful weather. "You know how you're always asking me trivia questions?"

"Yeah," I answered. It seemed as if I was into trivia more than ever. Now that Brian was coming over to see me so often, I was always trying to come up with great new bits of trivia to stump him. I couldn't resist trying out a few on Ally.

"Well, I've got one for you."

That was new! "I'm warning you," I said with a laugh. "I know just about everything. That trivia book Brian gave me for Christmas has 896 pages!"

"Do you know how many sisters there are in the world like you?" Ally asked.

That sounded like a trick question to me. "No, I don't know," I answered. "How many?"

"None," Ally said with a smile. "None."

About the Author

ALIDA E. YOUNG lives with her husband in the high desert of southern California. When she's not writing or researching a new novel, she enjoys taking long walks in the desert. To help her write her novels, she likes to put herself in the shoes of her characters, to try to feel things the way they would. Alida tries to feel all the pain and hurt, as well as all the joy and happiness, of her characters. When she's writing a book that requires research, such as *Is My Sister Dying?*, she talks to many different experts. "Everyone is so helpful," explains Alida. "They go out of their way to help."

Other books by Alida include *Summer Cruise, Summer Love, I Never Got to Say Good-bye,* and the Megan the Klutz books.